THE MAN WHO CROSSED WHIMSY AVENUE

AND 95 OTHER BITS OF FLASH FICTION

WARREN BLUHM

WARRENBLUHM.COM

CONTENTS

THE MAN WHO CROSSED WHIMSY AVENUE

and 95 other bits of flash fiction

Cover image "Whimsy Street" © Tetiana Kreminska| dreamstime.com

Virtually all of these stories originally appeared at warrenbluhm.com. Several also have been published in previous books. "The Accountant" was published in 2020 in *How to Play a Blue Guitar,* while "Jasper," "The Sudden Waltz," "The Monster Under the Bed," "Something Goes Horribly Wrong," "Chance Encounter at a Park Bench," "The Man by the Window," "The Room," "The wings," "The Story of the Cow, the Moose, and the Gnome on the Shelf," "The Newcomer," "Henry Saves the World," "No News is Good News," "Prologue to the Monarchs," "The Rest and the Dead," "The Room After Life," "Moose, Gnome and Cow Meet a Squirrel," "Beware the Idea," "Lovely Rita," "The Man Who Was Afraid of Finishing," and "The Place Holder" were included in *24 flashes,* the 2021 earlier edition of this book.

ISBN 978-0-9910107-0-7

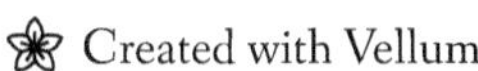 Created with Vellum

INTRODUCTION: THREE PARAGRAPHS AND A POSTSCRIPT

It seems I do my best work in miniature — "fragments of thoughts and bursts of creativity," as I once subtitled my blog. It probably has something to do with starting my career writing for radio news — I got used to telling several stories concisely enough to fit into three-minute newscasts.

The luxurious detail and intricate plot lines of short stories and novels do not come easily to me. Still, every so often a random scene springs from my imagination long enough to leave an impression.

It turns out that this sort of short-short story even has a name: flash fiction. Some of the little stories in this collection may even be too long to qualify as flash fiction, but I don't know what else to call them, so here they are.

P.S. I wrote the above three paragraphs several weeks ago and delayed finishing this book until I had more to say. I asked myself, "Does the book even need an introduction?" My self replied, "I love the introductions to Ray Bradbury's short-story collections," and so I waited to see if I had more to say. Finally I realized it's more important to get these little flashes to you than it is to write some high-falootin' introduction. And this is already longer than some of the stories that follow, so I'm going to make due with three paragraphs and a postscript.

Warren Bluhm
February 2025

IRONIC AIN'T IT

He took a deep breath.

"Here goes nothing," he said.

"You got that right," she said.

"What?"

"How long have I known you?" she said. "You always say, 'Here goes nothing,' and that's what comes out. Nothing ever comes of it."

"Now, that's just mean," he said.

"Not intentionally," she said. "All I'm saying is stop saying, 'Here goes.' Just go. Just do something or don't, you know, like Yoda says."

THE SUDDEN WALTZ

I always wondered where I would be today if I had stopped to tie my shoe and did not, after all, bump into her as I entered the store. I would have arrived five seconds later, and she would have already walked out the door and started up the street in the other direction.

Or I wonder where I would be today if she had been in a different mood and, when I bumped into her and asked her pardon, she would have said, "Watch where you're going, moron," instead of giggling and saying, "Shall we dance?" while grabbing my hand to keep her balance, which led to my swinging her around in a makeshift waltz.

Seventy years later, still holding hands, I'm glad I didn't stop to tie my shoe, even though the sudden waltz ended when I tripped.

ONCE UPON A HUG

The first thing he heard when he woke up that morning was a gentle voice saying, "Good morning, sleepyhead."

He turned toward the sound, propped himself up on one elbow and looked down at the face of a beautiful woman.

"Good morning, smile," he said softly.

He leaned down and kissed her cheek, then pulled up to look in her eyes.

They held that gaze for a moment, shining eyes into shining eyes, and then she smirked and said, "I know what you want."

"Oh, yeah?" he said.

"Yeah," she said and snuggled closer.

"What I want is to stay like this forever," he said, "because there's nothing sweeter than propping up on an elbow and looking into the eyes of the most beautiful woman who ever gave me the time of day."

"Oh," she said, still smiling.

"What did you think I wanted?"

"Never mind," she said. "I like your answer better."

They put their arms around each other, and with apologies to William Goldman, since the invention of the hug, there have been five hugs that were rated the most passionate, the most pure. This one left them all behind.

OPENING TO A SHORT STORY SET ON A SPACE STATION THREE-QUARTERS OF THE WAY TO THE MOON

The shuttle from Halfway Station was exactly on time, and he marveled at the precision needed to do that. A quarter of the distance between the Earth and the moon, measured in thousands of miles or kilometers or whatever, and the shuttle docked at 4:32 a.m. Greenwich Time, just as the schedule indicated.

Only three people disembarked, and a couple dozen boarded. Not many people stopped at Station 3/4. Who wants to live, work or play three-quarters of the way to the moon? Michael Collins had a great view, but who aspires to be the one in three who did not get to step on another heavenly body?

The woman who left the shuttle smiled when she saw him, and he returned the smile.

"Fancy meeting you here," she greeted him.

"Been a long time," he rejoindered.

They hugged, and it was like years had not passed. Surely she noticed he was thinner, a bit more frail, but she felt the same as ever in his arms. Why did he ever choose this life?

"So this is 3/4," she said.

"Not much to see."

"I wouldn't say that. It's cozy. Do you know what it takes to build something cozy 300,000 kilometers from Earth?"

"That does make it sound impressive," he admitted and could not resist adding, "but it wasn't very cozy until you arrived."

She rolled her eyes and laughed, and his mind was on a seashore in the sun, a warm breeze mingling that laugh with the cries of gulls overhead.

"It's good to see you," he said, and meant it.

"It's good to be seen," she said automatically, paused, and looked in his eyes. She touched his arm. "I mean it. I'm so glad to see you."

A long pause. A deep breath.

"Well, let's get your baggage and go get you settled."

BRIEF ENCOUNTER OF
THE ODD KIND

A long time ago in a place about 15 yards away ...
Nothing. Nothing happened. No one was there. I would love to tell you this was the place where a great adventure began, an epic of galactic proportions, perhaps even intergalactic.

But no, this is a nondescript place in an admittedly lovely countryside, but history has not marked it as any especially special place.

Wait a minute.

There is something there now that wasn't there before, a vehicle about the size of a semitrailer truck. I'm going out to see.

* * *

"What are you reading?"

"It's his journal. Take a look," she said, handing him the book. "Check the last entry."

He read quickly, then glanced up and around, his eyes doing a 360-degree turn focused about 15 yards away.

"I don't see anything, either," she said.

"You'd think there'd be some evidence that a semi was parked somewhere around here."

"He wrote 'about the size of' a semi. Who knows what that could mean?"

"Still," he said, "wouldn't there be some evidence of something that big? At least a depression in the grass?"

"You'd think so," she said. "I'm really worried. He writes in that book every day without fail, and that entry is dated four days ago."

Just then, both of them got a text alert, and they automatically withdrew their phones and stared at the screens.

"It's from him!" they shouted simultaneously.

"I suppose you're concerned. Don't be," said the text. "It's awesome out here."

Confused, they stared at each other, then up at the sky. It was a clear, quiet night, and countless stars coated the black with their faraway light.

TWO MUGS IN A BAR

Two mugs in a bar — kind of an old bar, somewhat clean, but you know how hard it is to get an old bar squeaky clean. Maybe they're old friends, or maybe they just happen to be sitting within earshot of each other at this particular moment.

The news is on TV, or maybe it's some politicians arguing over what the gummint should or should not do and how people can't be trusted so this has to stop.

One mug rolls his eyes.

"You know what nobody says anymore?" he says to anyone who will listen, or maybe to himself.

The other mug stares forward. The bartender dries a glass down the way.

"You know what nobody says anymore?" the mug tries again.

The other mug stirs from his reverie. "I don't know," he says. What does nobody say?"

"'It's a free country.'"

The other mug waits for more. When it appears nothing more is coming, he says, "That's it?"

"Well, yeah."

"Nobody says 'It's a free country' anymore?"

"Nope," says the first mug. "Used to be a couple guys start arguing over this or that or another thing, and sooner or later one of 'em says, 'Ah, baloney, it's a free country, I got a right to think that way, ain't hurting no one.'"

"Yeah, so?"

"So people stopped having a right to think stuff," the first mug says. "Maybe it's not a free country anymore."

"Are you kidding? This is the freest country in the world," says the other mug.

"Maybe that ain't saying much anymore. I mean, that one guy got fired the other day just for saying something he was thinking, you know what I mean?"

"Oh, come on, that was really stupid what he said."

"Of course it was, but people say stupid stuff all the time, and nobody used to get fired over it."

"Maybe they should have been," the other mugs says.

"Really? Isn't a free country where you have the right to say something stupid and everyone else is free to tell him he's stupid?"

"Right," says the other mug, "and his boss has the right to fire him."

"Over that?"

"Over whatever he damn well pleases. That's why he's called the boss."

"The bosses call the shots," the first mug agrees.

"Damn straight."

"So it never was a free country."

"I suppose not, when you think of it that way."

"But were bosses always this touchy?" the mug says.

"Ah, probably."

"Seems like it used to be you had to slug the boss or steal from the company to get fired."

"That was then," says the other mug. "Gotta watch your step these days."

"So I'm right," says the first mug.

"What?" says the other mug.

"Nobody says 'It's a free country' anymore."

"Maybe nobody says it," the other mug says, "but it's still the freest country in the world."

"That ain't saying much."

"Oh, yeah?"

"Yeah."

"Can I get you another?" the bartender says, sensing a situation that needs defusing. The other mug picks up the empty glass, looks inside to make sure it's empty, and sets it back down.

"Sure," says the other mug. "Why not?"

The two of them stare at the television screen while the bartender pours fresh drinks. On the TV one of the talking heads says, "This country is the leader of the free world, and we're not going to stand for this."

The other mug grins triumphantly. "See? You were saying?"

The first mug grunts.

After a minute, the first mug says, "The Sox sure stunk up the joint last night, huh?"

"Tell me about it."

BRING ME BACK

"Bring me back," he cried in his sleep. "Bring me back."

"Floyd, wake up," said his groggy wife. "You're talking in your sleep."

"Oh. What? Yeah," Floyd said, as he responded to her entreaty and woke up. "Wow, that was so real."

"No, it wasn't," she said. "I saw. You were right here all along."

"You know what I mean, Jen. I was walking down the street in some city —"

"Sounds dark."

"No, it was a bright sunny day. And this guy comes up, grabs my arm, and says, 'Come with me,' and I says, 'I don't want to come with you, I got things to do,' and he just hangs on and says, 'Come with me.'"

"Where'd he take you?"

"Next thing I'm in a boat on some wild rapids, and the boat is going up and down, and I started yelling, 'Bring me back,' and then I woke up."

They lay in the dark for a minute.

"That's it?" Jen asked.

"What do you mean?"

"You were yelling like you'd had some terrible vision and had to get home to save your sanity."

"Well, it was kind of scary, but nope, that's it. Walking down the street, strange guy, wild rapids on a crazy river."

"I thought you were going to tell me something like the strange guy introduced you to some mysterious organization that set you up to go on a mission only you could do, like rescue your long lost twin brother from a foreign prison, and you had to break into the prison and sneak around trying to avoid detection until you could nab him from his cell — or maybe you plucked him from the yard during recess — and then the two of you fooled the guards into thinking he was you and you were him, but you got captured, and the strange guy who grabbed you off the street was disguised as a guard and rescued you, and when he asked you if you wanted to work for him full-time, you said, 'No, bring me back, bring me back.'"

Floyd turned to his wife in the dark and slipped on hand under her and folded the other hand around her. They hugged for a moment and then unclenched.

"That would have been awesome, but that's your dream," he said. "I guess your dreams are more fun than mine."

They lay in the dark a few more minutes.

"I wonder who the guy represents," Jen said.

"Just some guy."

"Why did he throw you in the river?"

"I don't know how I got in the river," he said. "Maybe I escaped him and jumped in a boat."

"That's the thing about dreams," she said. "They don't make sense."

"Oh, someone would try to analyze it for me."

"That's all horse dookey," she said.

Floyd pondered that for a while.

"You're probably right," he said, leaned over and pecked Jen on the cheek. "I'm sorry to wake you."

They said their good nights and went back to sleep.

The autopsy showed that Floyd drowned. Jen was cleared of wrongdoing. The mystery was never solved, and she always wished he had dreamed her dream.

SASHA SAVES THE DAY

(B*ased on a true story.)*
Onyah and Sasha were pals. They lived with their people parents at their houses in the woods.

Onyah would run and play with Sasha like a puppy because, well, Onyah WAS a puppy.

"Be careful," Sasha would say, because she was older and wiser, "or one day you'll run and play right into trouble."

"You silly worry wart," Onyah would say. "Don't you worry about me."

One day in winter when the sun was shining but snow was on the ground, Mama Red let Onyah outside, and the little puppy went running in the woods near their home. She found a pond that was covered with ice.

Onyah walked on the ice and said, "Whee! It's slippery!!" And she ran and slid on the ice, crying, "Wheeeee!"

But all of a sudden, the ice went CRACK!

And Onyah went SPLASH! into a hole full of cold cold water.

Onyah tried to climb out, but her little paws weren't strong enough, and all she could do was put her paws on the edge of the ice and cry.

"On-yah! Come inside now!" Mama Red called from the house. "Where are you?"

Just then Sasha and her humans, Jim and Heidi, were taking a walk along the road. Mama Red came out to see them.

"Have you seen Onyah? She didn't come when I called, and I'm worried," Mama Red said.

"Oh dear," said Heidi. "Let's go look for her."

After a few minutes, Sasha heard cries from somewhere and ran up a little hill.

"What is it, Sasha?" Jim said. "What do you see over the hill?"

He walked up behind Sasha and saw Onyah's sad little face with her paws hanging onto the ice.

"Oh my!" Jim said, and he ran over, stretched himself out on the ice, and grabbed Onyah's little paws.

He pulled her gently out of the water and hugged her tight, to warm her back up.

"What a good girl Sasha is!" said Mama Red. "And what a sassy dog you are, Onyah!"

They took both dogs home and laid them next to the fire.

"I told you," Sasha scolded Onyah. "One day you were going to run right into trouble, and today was the day."

"You were right," Onyah said sadly. "I will be careful from now on."

"That's good," Sasha said. "After all, my humans and I may not always be there to save you."

"But you did save me!" Onyah cried. "Oh, Sasha, we will always be pals!"

WILLOW FINDS A HOME

(B*ased on a true story.*)

Once upon a time, in the Land of Wisconsin, in the County of Door, a good noble dog we'll call Goldie gave birth to six puppies. There was Willie and Walter, and WoWo and Wilma, and Wooster and Willow, and they were the sweetest golden puppies you ever did see.

They played and they played, and they ran and they ran, and they lived on a farm where Belgians had worked the land for more than a hundred years.

They started as puppies and grew to be pups on the way to becoming good dogs. Soon it was time to find forever homes and families for them and say goodbye to Goldie. First WoWo went away, and then Walter found a home, and Wooster went west, and Willie went east, and finally one day it was just Wilma and Willow, and a good little girl picked up Wilma and squealed, "She's so sweet! Let's take her home."

"Don't worry, Willow," Wilma called out to her sister. "Someone will come for you any day now."

"I know," Willow said, but she wasn't so sure. And the days

went by and Willow stayed with Goldie but she missed her little brothers and sisters and felt all alone.

And then one day a tall guy and a short sweet lady came to the farm to look for a pup. The farmer met them at the barn door.

"Well, we have just one 6-week-old pup left and a pile of 4-week-old puppies, you can have your pick," said the farmer.

"OK, let's see the older one first," said the short sweet lady. "We just lost our Onyah, and there's a hole in our hearts for a puppy to fill just as soon as we can."

"We even picked out a name for her," said the tall guy, reaching into the box and picking up the lonely little girl with both hands.

She looked up into his eyes, and he held her gentle as can be, and she snuggled right in and decided right then and there that he was very nice.

And then he asked something that made her all goosebumpy.

"Are you Willow?" he said. "We picked out a name, and we came here to take Willow home."

How did he know? Oh, how did he know! "Yes, I am Willow," she would have said, except his gentle hands were putting her to sleep. She curled up in his hands and rested her head on his chest, and she knew she was home. She was home!

"Here," the tall guy said to the short sweet lady, "I'm pretty sure this is Willow," and handed her over.

"Oh, aren't you the cutest puppy ever!" said the short sweet lady with a big smile. "You're such a pretty girl, sure you are." And Willow melted in her hands, too.

"Want to look at the 4-week-olds now?" asked the farmer.

"No!" cried the tall guy.

"No!" cried the short sweet lady.

"This is Willow," said the tall guy.

"Yes, this is Willow," said the short sweet lady.

How did they know? How did they know! Willow didn't care, she was just happy she was going home with them.

And she put her paw on the tall guy's chest and sank back in with a soft yawn, and somehow she knew she was going to live happily ever after.

THE MAN WHO CROSSED WHIMSY AVENUE

A man was walking along, deep in thought, lost in worries about this and that and another thing, when suddenly he realized he had stumbled into a wonderland.

Everything was bright colors and magic buses and this can't be real, but it was real enough and whimsically nonsensical.

"You there!" cried a friendly enough looking police officer. "Why are you dressed so drably? Why aren't you smiling? Are you quite all right?"

"I'm not sure," said the man. "Where is this?"

"Ah, it's another one," the officer said gently. "You were walking along all worried, right?"

"I don't see how that's anyone's —"

"Right, right, right," smiled the officer. "That's absolutely correct, it's not my business. Well enough. You just didn't notice you'd crossed Whimsy Avenue. No worries, you're going to be fine, move along."

And the officer walked away. Now the man looked around and saw that, no matter where he looked, he saw something impossibly amazing.

"Here now, watch where you're going," said a cat with a cockney accent in a tuxedo.

"Woof," said a friendly dog who sniffed at his hand and looked around for balls.

Above, the sky was orange — not the majestic orange of a setting sun, but the orange of an orange (you know, the fruit) or construction paper.

"I can show you the way to Normal," huffed a gray-haired woman in glasses, "but you won't like it there, not ever again."

And that was the beginning of a beautiful friendship. It seemed the woman had been a tense old thing until one day she happened upon Whimsy Avenue — although she found some people called it Whimsy Street, for some reason — and she never looked back, although she did still tend to fuss about.

"Don't mind me, I'm just an old fuss bucket. No harm intended," she would tell people.

There may be some tales to tell about the man and the fussy gray-haired woman on Whimsy Avenue, if I can find my way back there myself ...

BARNABY CAPSIS

"When my brain is clear, the pathways feel so snappy!" Barnaby Capsis cried not long after he awoke one morning, to no one in particular, as he lived alone.

Barnaby woke that day with all his synapses snapping like firecrackers. He could feel his mind snap-crackling and popping as if anything could happen, and, of course, it did.

As he was walking down the street, a woman he thought he'd never seen before called, "Barnaby Capsis!" He watched as she walked up to him as if she had a purpose, which, of course, she did.

"Barnaby, you're just the man I'm looking for," she said.

"Oh," he replied, not quite snappily. "What can I do for you?"

And the answer to that question changed everything. Answers always change something, but in this case it changed everything, because of the wonderful whiz he was.

Now, you may ask, why the woman could possibly need Barnaby, and how helping her could possibly change not anything but everything.

"Changing everything" could mean that they are destined to live happily ever after together, but perhaps that's too much a cliche. On another hand, "changing everything" could mean that she needs him to go on a hero's journey that will change not just Barnaby but the whole world he lives in, but then it's a big story and not just a bit of fluff.

As it happens, when Barnaby asked, "What can I do for you?" she smiled slyly, one of those smiles that says how delighted the smiler is to be asked that precise question, while also suggesting that the smilee may not realize how big a question that is.

And, the smile still in her eyes, she frowned and answered his question.

"That's all, in point of fact," she said. "I wanted to tell you you're just the man I'm looking for."

"Yes," Barnaby said, a tad confused, "but why were you looking for me?"

"Do I need a reason to be looking for a man?"

"Ah! But then, why have you decided I am that man?"

The frown that disguised the sly smile now broke into a full grin.

"I knew you were the man I needed," she laughed. "Your synapses are surely snapping today, aren't they?"

He rose up a bit at that. "I'm not sure the condition of my synapses are any of your business, but yes, I do feel a bit snappy today."

"Snappy in a good way, of course?"

"Of course."

"Good! Then come with me."

She turned with a flourish, took his hand, and stepped away, but he did not step with her.

"Hang on! Where are we going?"

And she gave him that sly smile, which proved irresistible, and headed hand-in-hand down the street. He had to admit the warmth of her hand in his was comfortable, reassuring, and vaguely familiar, although he did not admit this out loud.

They walked that way for several blocks in silence, until they came to a city park, which should not be surprising because this was a very green city full of parks every few blocks, and the parks resembled each other in that they were full of grass and trees and sidewalks with benches and people who enjoyed a bit of greenery in their cities.

She detached her hand and walked slowly, less purposefully, by his side, still quiet for a few moments, so it was almost a surprise when she finally spoke.

"I need your help."

"I see," Barnaby said. "So when you said, 'You're just the man I'm looking for,' you were being more specific after all?"

She laughed, and he decided then and there that he liked her laugh and, indeed, was on his way to liking her.

"We may someday decide that it was a more general statement, but yes, for today I need someone whose synapses are snapping like angry turtles."

"I'm not angry."

"I know," she said. "It's a simile."

"Or a metaphor?" Barnaby said hopefully.

"No, there's a difference. This was a simile."

"All right. What do you need my synapses for?"

Just then a villainous-looking villain appeared at the edge of the clearing.

"Aha!" said the villain. "This is what you do when I'm not watching you."

"Oh, no!" She said, and then to the villain, "What do you expect? You are a villainous villain!"

"And what's your part in this — Barnaby Capsis, isn't it?"

"Why, yes," Barnaby said modestly, "but she was about to tell me what my part is. As it is, I don't even know her name."

"It's Delia," the woman said softly.

"I'm pleased to meet you," said Barnaby Capsis. "Do you wish me to escort this villain off the premises?"

"If only it were that easy! No, I was hoping you could help me conjure an escape."

"Never!" cried the villain, but then he disappeared in a puff of smoke.

"What the —?" Barnaby and Delia said in unison.

Delia threw her arms around Barnaby and hugged him fiercely.

"You saved my life!" she cried.

"But how?"

"Does it matter?" she whispered. "You are just the man I was looking for."

The mystery was never solved, but they lived happily ever after. Some things are just mysterious like that.

THE ACCOUNTANT

"Fear is the mind killer, fear is the mind killer, fear is the mind killer—shit!" he spat, cowering behind the dumpster with his ears wide open for signs of approaching footsteps.

Why hadn't he seen this coming? All of the signs were there—the precocious co-worker suddenly gone silent, the whispers and glances as he passed in the hallway, the emails and calls not returned. No time to think about all that now, though—all that mattered was getting out of this alley alive.

He risked a glance around the corner of the giant garbage container. The alley was empty that way, and he could see no one between here and the other end.

"No time like the present," a brave-sounding peep emerged from his throat. He stood and ran.

He ran with all of his might, and he could feel stabs of pain in his arthritic hip. No time for that, gotta run – run – run – run – RUN!

He heard the click of a door beginning to open behind him as he emerged from the alley, so he took a sharp turn down the sidewalk and eased his pace to a brisk walk. No way whoever was opening the door would have been able to see before he was around the corner, right? Right? He kept walking just in case, blending into the crowd, and didn't look back.

A block. Two blocks. Three blocks.

There. Free and clear! He was out of there. All of the obstacles he had seen in front of him were imaginary, or overcome. He was out, safe and sound. All of his fears were—

"Bob?"

His heart froze. He looked around.

"I thought that was you. Hi, Bob. It's good to see you."

He eyed the older-looking man cautiously.

"Sam. Sam Lopez. From school."

Bob relaxed, slightly.

"Oh, hi, Sam." And then with more feeling, remembering and recognizing. "Sam! Yes, of course. How are you?"

"Doing great. Got a little family started, got work as an accountant."

"That's terrific."

"How about you?"

"Oh," and Bob's heart resumed its racing. "I'm—I'm between jobs right now, looking for opportunities, as they say," with a slight forced laugh. "Sorry I have to hit and run, Sam, but I have a thing I have to get to."

"Sure, Bob, I understand," Sam said, reaching into his jacket.

The gun was out and fired twice so quickly that Bob barely had time to register he was going to be shot. He felt the impact but not the pain, even after blood began to sprout from his chest.

"I'm sorry, Bob," Sam said kindly. "There had to be an accounting."

THE MONSTER UNDER THE BED

"I'm the monster under the bed," the boy cried.

"That's nice," said Mom. "What makes you a monster?"

"Well, I – I roar and I scare little boys."

"You ARE a little boy," she said. "Do you scare yourself?"

He looked thoughtful. "Sometimes."

This gave Mom pause.

"Why do you scare yourself?"

"Well – that's what monsters do! I wouldn't be much of a monster if I didn't scare myself sometimes."

"OK, how do you scare people?"

"I don't want to scare YOU, Mom."

"Oh, come on, I like being scared."

"You do?"

"It can be fun."

"Well – I eat them."

"You eat people?"

"Yep."

"How do you get your mouth big enough to eat someone?"

"I think that's what scares them."

"Oh, this I gotta see."

"I don't wanna."

"Come on, son, scare me."

"You won't like it."

"I promise, I'll like it. It sounds cute."

"Well, OK."

Dad came home a few hours later.

"Where's Mom?" he asked the little boy, who shrugged and crawled under the bed.

"What are you doing under the bed, son?"

"Come see."

PRINCESS AND PIE

Once upon a time there was this place. No one could reach the princess when she was there, so she went there often. It wasn't that she didn't love being a princess or serving her people; she just liked to be alone in her quiet place sometimes. It helped her think, it helped her rest, and it helped her understand what needed to be done.

One day she was in her place when a man on a flaming pie appeared.

"Oh! How did you get here?" cried the princess. "No one can reach me in this place."

"And yet here I am, said the man. "I'm surprised that you didn't ask me who I am first."

"I don't care who you are," she said. "This is where I go when I don't wish to be disturbed."

"If I am disturbing you —"

"Of course you are."

"— then I apologize," he said. "But I have an important message that —"

"Can't it wait?"

"—cannot wait."

"Well, then," the princess huffed. "What is it?"

"Do you see this flaming pie?"

"You're standing on it," she said. "How could I not?"

"Yes, well," the man said, "it brings tidings of great suffering across the land."

"A flaming pie is an harbinger of doom?"

"Scoff if you like, milady," said the man, "but flaming pies are rare and important messengers."

"Oh, such as 'You shall be Beatles with an A'?"

"Ah, you've heard that one."

"'Rare and important'?"

"Imagine if they were merely Beetles."

"Must I?"

"No, you mustn't," he said. "That is, you may if you like, but it is not required. But this message does indeed affect the entire kingdom."

"We have no king," said the princess.

"Whatever you wish to call the land," the man said, "the flaming pie says it is imperiled."

"Do tell," said the princess, skeptically.

"On the 17th day of the 17th month after the cloudy moon, a rebel will arise to end the monarchy as we know it."

"And how does this rebel intend to end the monarchy?"

"The pie is vague on that point," the man said. "It only wishes to sound the warning, and one other clue: The rebel will gather strength from the monolith at Dubyedodown Down."

"I think you're mad," the princess said. "There is nothing to be found at Dubyedodown Down but geese and random toads."

"Nevertheless, the revolution will begin there, on the 17th day of the 17th month after the cloudy moon."

"Yes, yes, but I must return to my quiet now," said the princess. "When was the last cloudy moon anyway?"

The flaming pie lifted the man into the sky, but as he rose out of sight he called, "Seventeen months and 16 days ago."

"So," she replied, "the rebel arrives tomorrow?"

But the man on the flaming pie was gone and could not answer or, if he could, could not be heard.

The princess pondered this vision and the message for many minutes, and then she emerged from her quiet place, not at all alarmed but a tad wary. Who was the man on the flaming pie, and how had he encroached on her quiet place? Who was this rebel? And how could one rebel break up the monarchy from down Dubyedodown Down? It seemed so very hard to do.

Still, she knew it could be true, and began to make precautions.

CUTENESS EVERSWEET

Cuteness Eversweet drew back her bow and eyed the target carefully. A hummingbird buzzed around a lilac bush.

Cuteness let the arrow fly, and a moment later a sudden shaft protruded from the center of a bull's eye planted under a tree. Startled, the hummingbird darted away.

"Oh, I'm sorry, little one," she said. "Don't worry, no one's going to hurt you on my watch."

Cuteness Eversweet loved all living things in equal measure. Well, fine, she did not apologize to carrots when she chopped and diced them. But Cuteness loved animals and was a diehard vegetarian. Her friends stopped inviting her to dinner because of the sad faces she made as they savored their ribeyes.

One day a hungry bear approached Cuteness Eversweet in the forest. She led the bear to a raspberry bush, then a beehive brimming with honey, but the bear kept eying Cuteness like her friends eyed juicy hamburgers.

"Can't we come to some agreement not to eat each other?" Cuteness Eversweet asked.

"Let me think about that for a second," said the bear. "Um — no."

So Cuteness sadly picked up a large stick and clubbed the bear on the side of his head. The great beast dropped like a stone, unconscious.

"I suppose you're going to eat him now," said the hummingbird.

"Goodness, no, of course not," said Cuteness Eversweet.

"But I am," said a hunter who suddenly appeared, wielding a great hunting knife with which to dispatch the bear.

Before he could do any such thing, however, Cuteness bashed him in the side of the head, too.

Now she had a dilemma: Two carnivores, side by side, unconscious, and likely more than willing to devour each other once they awoke. Also, both of them were too big for her to drag one or the other to safety.

She set to work with rope that the archery range coincidentally had stockpiled in its storage shed, and when they awoke the bear and the hunter were surprised to find themselves securely tied.

"If I release you, I want you both to walk away and leave the other in peace," Cuteness told them.

"Are you crazy? I'm a hunter," said the hunter. "I shoot bears."

"And I'm a bear," said the bear. "I eat people."

"I sincerely wish you would not," said Cuteness Eversweet.

"Yeah, well, if wishes were horses, then beggars would ride," said the bear.

Suddenly a horse appeared, and a huge white-haired bearded man dismounted.

"Why it's Duke X. Machina," cried the hunter.

"That's me," said the duke. "And you two must depart these woods in peace, for I have so decreed.

Grumbling, the hunter and the bear skulked away in opposite directions.

"Thank you for resolving my dilemma, Duke," Cuteness Eversweet said gratefully.

"It was my pleasure, milady," said Duke X. Machina.

"I love a happy ending," the hummingbird hummed.

And come to think of it, they all did live happily ever after.

LOVE AND MAGIC

Once upon a time, in a kingdom so magical it was called The Magic Kingdom — but that name was spoken only in whispers because of trademark issues — the magical king and the magical queen were having a tiff.

Now, a tiff is a little more serious than a disagreement but less serious than a row, but the thing about disagreements is they can lead to a tiff, and the thing about a tiff is they can lead to a row, so the best course is to settle things before one thing leads to another.

And so the magical daughter stepped in to say, "Mother, Father, please don't let this tiff spoil this magical day. Surely you can find common ground or a middle solution."

"How can such a big problem have a little solution?" asked the king, who was hard of hearing.

"You old coot, she said 'middle' with an M," the queen sputtered. "And how can you say this is a big problem? It's fiddlesticks and froo fram.

"So you've been saying," the king muttered. "You never listen to me."

On they sputtered and muttered until they were all puttered out. Then they smiled at each other and held hands.

"That's better!" cried the magical daughter. "I'm so glad that's settled."

"We haven't settled anything," said the king.

"But you're holding hands," the daughter said. "You have your love, and love settles everything."

"You are still young, and learning," said the queen, "and have not yet learned that sometimes love isn't enough."

"Oh, but you are old, and forgetful," the daughter replied, "and what you have forgotten is that love is all you need."

At that the king leaned over and purred something into the queen's ear that made her giggle. She kissed him, and he kissed her, and they wrapped their arms around each other, and quickly they both forgot what the tiff was about in the first place.

"Perhaps you should get a room," suggested the magical daughter.

And so, they did.

TWO COWS ON A SHELF

The cows smiled as they surveyed all that they could survey. It was a cluttered panorama with papers and wires scattered everywhere but, paradoxically, books arranged in a certain order and movie posters neatly placed on the wall.

"It's as if he can't make up his mind to be a cluttered mess or obsessive compulsive," one cow said to the other. The cows didn't have names because, as an impossible quasi super villain once said, they knew who they are.

"We must have an adventure," said the other cow.

"Why?"

"Well," said the adventurer, "there has to be a story to tell about us so people remember who we are."

"Why can't we be remembered as the two little cows who sat contentedly smiling on the bookshelf for years upon years and lived happily ever after?"

"Yes, I suppose we could," said the other. "But something has to happen to make it a story. That's what makes it a story: Things happen."

"I don't want anything to happen. It means change, and I like things just the way they are."

"So do I. But wouldn't an adventure be grand?"

"It depends on the adventure. Some are full of mystery and intrigue and peril, which are three things I'm not terribly fond of."

"I see what you mean," the other said. "But this could be an adventure of discovery and beauty and strange new worlds and new civilizations."

"I'm not sure I like 'strange.'"

"Now you're just being contrary. Come on, let's go."

"You go ahead. I'm happy right here."

"I'm not going anywhere without you. We are two peas in a pod."

"No, we're two cows on a shelf. And I like it that way."

"Oh, all right," the would-be adventurer conceded. "I was just saying."

"But you got your wish."

"I did?"

"Yes. We're in a story."

"But nothing happened!"

"Fancy that."

And they did live happily ever after.

THE GREAT AMERICAN SOMETHING

The program ended, and they looked at the clock.

"I must leave you now, love," he said. "I'm off to write The Great American Something."

"Oh," she said admiringly. "You're off to write a novel?"

"Perhaps. It will be Something, whatever it is. And Great. And American. Yes, indeed."

"I always knew you had it in you," she gushed.

"Yes, well," he said modestly.

He positioned himself at the keyboard, stared down the blinking cursor, and began.

"In a land beyond the horizon next to a big river, there was this city," he wrote. "But it is not of the city that I write, no, not that grand metropolis of hundreds of thousands of people, but one of its denizens, two actually."

There followed a heartbreaking saga of a man who loved a woman, and the woman who loved the man, and how they faced a challenge that they believed would crush them both, except that when they held each other's hands and faced it together, it turned out that nothing could stop them. It took a very long time and hundreds of pages of trials and tribulations before they realized this combined power, however, and by the time of their triumph, they were exhausted, but not too exhausted to spare a historic embrace and a legendary kiss, the kind of kiss that legends are made of.

And as he wrote the final page, tears streamed down his cheeks and he nodded to himself.

"Now this," he said, "is Something."

For he had set out to write The Great American Something, poured his soul into the keyboard, and Something indeed came out.

Years later, she looked at him one night with a thoughtful expression.

"What would you have done that night so long ago, when the program ended and you announced you were off to write The Great American Something —" she paused.

"Yes?"

"What if I had said, 'No, don't, stay here and let's spend the night together?'"

He looked in her eyes with a look that was looking very, very far away indeed.

"Why, I would have swept you into my arms and loved you all night for the rest of our lives," he said, "and there might never ever have been a Great American Something after all."

"I thought so," she said sadly and slyly. "I'm glad, then, that I didn't say what I was thinking."

"What!" he said. "You didn't want me to go away and write?"

"Oh, I did," she admitted, "but I mostly was thinking how lonely I would be while you were away."

"I'm so sorry!"

"I'm not," she said. "Because here it is now, The Great American Something, just as you envisioned, and here you are now, in my arms, just as I envisioned."

They held each other gently and firmly then, and it would be a cliche to say they lived happily ever after, but truth be told, sometimes a cliche describes a truth.

THE FABLE OF THE MAN WITH THE SQUIRREL ON HIS HEAD

Once there was a man with a squirrel on his head. He was walking along the sidewalk, minding his own business, when big old Betty Busybody sidled up to him and said, "Pssst! Did you know there's a squirrel on your head?"

Immediately the squirrel grabbed its own head with its front paws and said, "No, there's not!"

"Of course not," Betty said. "I was talking with this gentleman!"

"He's no gentleman!" said the squirrel.

"Now, now, let me speak for myself, my little pal," said the man.

"Yes, indeed," said Betty.

"By all means," said the squirrel.

"Thank you," the man said, and looked Betty in the eye fiercely. "Listen, you big old busybody, what's on my head is my own flipping business."

"Why, I never —" Betty began.

"Maybe you should have, once or twice," snarled the man with the squirrel on his head. And with that, he stalked away, leaving poor Betty behind, standing gobsmacked on the sidewalk.

"I told you," called the squirrel before they walked out of sight. "He's no gentleman."

MISSED OPPORTUNITIES

"Oh, Great Muse, who has inspired the creators through the aeons, settle over me and guide these hands to tell the story you would have me tell ..."

"Oh, please stop."

"Wait, what?"

"You're making me throw up in my mouth, and not just a little bit."

"Great Muse?"

"Who did you think you were calling, Louis Armstrong?"

"I don't know who that is."

"No, you don't, do you, and that's part of the problem, innit?"

"You don't have to be mean."

"Oh yes, child, yes I do. You think you can just plop yourself down, invoke a Muse you ignored for months, and get the goods right away? Are you really that stupid?"

"There's no need to be rude."

"Yes, actually there is. I've been nice and sweet and inspiring, and none of those approaches are working. So you know what? F

—- you, man. F—you and your 'Oh Great Muse' bulls—- I'm outta here."

There followed a long, deep silence, and then the writer said, "Huh."

And off he went to take a nap. While he was sleeping, someone else wrote the story.

MAD WORLD

T he ruler of the universe as we know it sat behind a desk cogitating. All was going as planned. The usual suspects had been rounded up, and now all that was necessary was to draft charges to justify the roundup.

An aide simpered into the room — Chad was his name, wasn't it?

"My Ruler, I humbly apologize, but I don't understand why we are rounding these people up."

The Ruler stared icily into the aide's eyes.

"There is much you don't know about these people, or you wouldn't be asking that question."

"All I've been able to learn is that they don't agree with your policies on —"

"And isn't that enough?" the Ruler snapped. "They are evil people who stand in the way of our glorious plans to save the people from themselves."

"They have the same goals as you, they just have different ideas about how to accomplish them."

"You dare to question my plan?"

"No, no, of course not. But they do," said the aide. "Some of them are good people, they just disagree —"

"Good people do not block the doors of the feeding house so others cannot eat."

"Yes, but they're not —"

"Don't you know these are greedy people who want to keep all the food for themselves?"

"They've never said —"

"If I had the power, I would wipe their selfish faces from the earth."

"They only disagree with you! They're not horrible people."

The Ruler paused in mid-rant and looked more carefully at the aide.

"How did you get in here? What fool hired you, of all people, to be one of my advisors?"

"Are you kidding, Ruler? You picked me, you Brough me on board, we've been friends for as long as I can remember."

"Yes, I recall now," said the Ruler. "You've changed so much, I hardly recognize you."

"What, me, change? Of course not. I helped draft the plan, I just don't understand why we have to arrest all these innocent people."

"INNOCENT?! Is that what you call those who object to the glorious plan?"

"They are conscientious objectors, not revolutionaries."

"And you know this how? Have you joined them after all this time?"

The aide appeared to want to speak, but chose to be silent.

"How may I serve my Ruler today?" the aide said after a long silence.

"By reporting to the guard outside the door and having him escort you to processing," the Ruler said. "I'm so disappointed in you, Chad."

"It's Brad," the aide said. "But it doesn't matter."

I PROCLAIM YES

In a world cowering behind a mighty wall of fear and anger, the Defiant One strode confidently into the arena. The crowd would have cheered, but the authorities had banned crowds.

He strutted pridefully to the center of the vast staging area and looked around at where the thousands of faces would have been.

"You have been told no. I proclaim yes," the Defiant One said.

"You have been told freedom is slavery. I declare freedom is freedom and slavery is slavery. Two plus two equals four. What you see is what you get.

"War is being waged for your mind, heart and soul. Or rather, war is being waged against your mind, heart and soul. The enemy wants you to be afraid and angry and frustrated and, most of all, the enemy wants you alone.

"But in that solitude is power — the power to isolate yourself from the mass and think for yourself. The mass hears the drone of the enemy's machine; the solitary soul, away from the drone, can hear the whispers of reality — a reality where ignorance is ignorance, strength is strength, war is war, and peace is peace – above all, peace is peace: Peace is freedom from fear and anger and frustration; peace is time enough to think, listening to the rhythms of calm and confidence and reassurance.

"Come then, follow the melody of your mind, heart and soul, follow the path that restores and does not ruin, the song that soothes and does not disparage, the words and music that build a bridge across troubled waters. Join in peace and friendship; seek understanding, not division. Defy the warlords and their threats clothed in empty promises. Enough cowering; stand in peace, stand for peace, drop the mask of suspicion and stand as individuals united against those who would strike terror in our hearts."

The arena echoed with the defiant words, for there was no crowd. But the words were heard, and soon it was the warlords who knew fear and anger and frustration, for no one would heed their calls to hate and violence, as the people looked at each other and saw common ground, not a chasm — love, not hate — freedom, not enemies.

LITERALLY CANT

The fairie looked back at the horse and grinned.

"You there, horse," said the fairie. "Have you ever seen the like?"

The horse gaped.

"Nope, not in this lifetime," said the horse. And if horses could smile, this horse would have.

Words can't describe the sight, so I can only describe their reaction. Both creatures broke into widey-wide smiles bigger than smiles are expected to be, and their hearts swelled with a mad joy, and they would spend the rest of their lives remembering the sight and unable to put it into words. They were forever grateful for having seen it, as would anyone.

What do you mean, what did they see? I refer you to the previous paragraph, the one that begins, "Words can't describe the sight." As I am using words, it should be clear that I am unable to describe what they saw. Oh, but they saw it, make no mistake, and they were forever changed. One woman smiled for the next 46 years that remained of her life.

And so, yes, if you ask if lives were changed that day, and for the better, yes, yes, yes.

Our lives need wonder, and on that day of all days, wonder was in abundance.

PLUS 2

"Excuse me, nurse? I'm here with Patient THX 1140, and he seems to have taken leave of his senses."

"What makes you say that?"

"Well, his senses are scattered here all over the floor, and there's no sign of him."

"Hmmm. That IS concerning."

"Concerning what?"

"It's concerning, that's all."

"Concerning what? Concerning Henry?"

"No, that's 'Regarding Henry' with Harrison Ford. And Patient THX 1140 is not named Henry."

"Of course not, he's named THX 1140 — it's a Lucas homage."

"Lucas Skywalker?"

"No, that's someone else entirely."

"Oh! The horse of a different color you've heard tell about?"

"Now you're in Oz."

"Wouldn't you be?"

"No, I'd eat ivy, too. Wouldn't you?"

"Oh, get that boy under control."

"Why?"

"Why?! Because control is what it's all about."

"You're a control freak?"

"No, you are."

"No, you are."

"No, you are."

"Well, one of us is."

"Or both."

"Or neither."

"You're talking to yourself as if you're two people."

"Three."

"What?"

"Id, ego, superego."

"You're a Jung man, then."

"No, actually I'm officially old now."

"What the actual F—"

"Now, now, now!"

"Here and now?"

"Just now. That's all we have."

"Got that right."

"Left right left."

"How did we get here?"

"Wouldn't you like to know?"

"No."

FROM THE NORTH IT COMES

"You have to inject yourself with a little fantasy every day in order not to die of reality." — The Ray Bradbury Facebook page posted that quote Wednesday.

So here I am at my desk, fixing to write the Great American Novel, working on a Great American Newspaper, generally doing Great American Work.

I have little choice but to do American work, seeing as I am second-generation American by birth, being the grandson of immigrants (except for the quarter whose grandmother was in Daughters of the American Revolution). You may hyphenate me as you will, but I was born in America to parents who were born in America, so there you have it.

And what is "American"? That seems to depend on who you ask, and most Americans seem to think "American" is what agrees with their personal opinion — and so it is.

Superman was once said to stand for truth, justice and the American way, and all three of those subjects are open to interpretation these days.

So will I produce a Great American Novel or a Great American Newspaper? Any greatness in or around me is not for me to say anyway, so I don't spend much time thinking about it. I just put down the words as I have the time and see fit, and the rest of you can take it from there.

And what does this have to do with injecting ourselves with a little fantasy today?

I'm not actually sure. I think I should be less concerned about truth and justice and more concerned about what that dragon is doing in my backyard. It seems friendly enough; it even pranced and danced with our dogs like they were old friends.

Every so often, the dragon looks to the north skies as if expecting a bad storm, either a late winter blizzard or an early spring thunderstorm capable of spawning tornadoes. But from its body language and its vigilance, I really don't think it's concerned about anything Mother Nature could throw at us.

No, I think the dragon is watching for something manmade, or perhaps something supernatural, but whatever it is, I'm pretty sure it's something evil.

I wonder if there are any Scarecrows, Tin Men or even a cowardly lion in the neighborhood.

VIGIL

I never noticed before how much a dragon resembles a giraffe. The long snout, the snaky neck — the only difference is that one has cute fuzzy markings and the other is scaly and reptilian. Oh, and the wings.

As I said last night, the dragon in our backyard is friendly enough. Dejah and Summer — especially Summer, the 1-year-old — love to play with it. They dart around its legs and sniff nuzzle-to-nose like kittens around a doting aunt. The dragon seems to sense it could smash our golden retrievers without a thought, and so it is always conscious and thoughtful as they frolic together.

What is it that troubles the dragon so? As soon as the dogs come inside, the dragon sits and resumes its vigil. Always, its eyes scan the sky and the horizon to the north, as if it knows what it expects to see and is ready to meet whatever that threat is.

I feel the threat may be imminent, but it just as easily could be months or even years off. And why did the dragon choose our backyard to prepare its stand? Is this simply a strategic location — hard to believe because, while we are on a hill, there is higher ground above us — or is there something special about this home or its occupants? Surely we are just an average and ordinary older couple. Our retrievers are sweet and loving, but most retrievers are. Could it be the cat? Could there be something valuably mystical about a black cat of 15 years that yowls incessantly day and night? Are the yowls a warning against the danger the dragon awaits?

What can all this mean? Why is the dragon here? What is the yowling about? Part of me prays this vigil will not become some apocryphal battle until after we are safely departed to the next world or our just desserts, whichever is more pleasant. Part of me realizes it's more likely we have been chosen to stand this ground and help the dragon defend against whatever is coming.

I have no idea what that is — what menace would I need a dragon's help to fight? Why here? And why now, if indeed it will be now? All that seems certain is it's coming from the north and that its existence troubles an otherwise friendly and playful dragon.

And so, like refugees in Casablanca during other troubled times, we wait — and wait — and wait — and wait.

CHANCE ENCOUNTER AT A PARK BENCH

Winston looked both ways and behind him before he started to write.

"I think the Marxists are about to topple the government. Either they will win the election, or they will take it forcefully afterward rather than concede defeat. The rioting is just the precursor, legitimizing their violence in the streets ..."

"Whatcha got there?"

"Wha—" Winston jumped up from the park bench and stepped away from the stranger, who assessed him curiously. "Where did you come from?"

"I saw you writing and wanted to take a peek at what was so interesting, is all."

"Do you always sneak up on people and look at what they're writing? I should report you to —"

"But you won't, will you? It's too risky."

"What's that supposed to mean?"

"Well, you know," said the stranger. "You report me checking out what you were writing, and they're going to want to read it, too. What was so interesting that I had to see it, and when they see it, well — you know."

"There's nothing illegal about what I was writing," Winston said, clutching the journal to his chest.

"I know that, maybe. But is it something you'd want people to know you were thinking? You sure seem to be a little jumpy about it."

"I'm jumpy because someone snuck up behind me and scared me."

"So you say," the stranger said. "But, like I said, they're still going to want to know why you were scared someone would read your journal."

The two men regarded each other warily.

"Why did you decide to spy on me?" Winston asked after a moment.

"Why are you so defensive about it?"

"I'm not being defensive. It's just that normal people don't poke their nose into other people's books, people they don't know."

"Granted," said the stranger. Another pause. "Can I trust you?"

"What kind of a question is that? You don't know me, and I don't know you."

"Well, actually," a chuckle, "I overheard you the other day at the cafe, the Ishtar's Nest? The riots were on TV, and I heard what you said to your friend about the —" a whisper now — "Marxists."

Winston's eyes widened.

"I don't know what you're —"

"Yes, you don't know what I'm talking about, very good, very good. I just want you to know you're not alone."

"Are you saying —"

"Yes. You're not alone," the stranger said. "Many people feel the same way."

"There are more like you?"

"Like us, yes," the stranger nodded significantly.

"How do I know you're not one of them, trying to trick me?"

"You don't, but I'm not. The rioters must be stopped," the other said. "We are meeting tonight in the warehouse district to discuss what to do about the problem."

"Yes?" Winston said, gently touching the stranger's forearm. "When? Where?"

"11 o'clock," the man said, and gave an address. "Shall I see you then?"

"Yes."

The stranger strolled away into the park. Mourning doves cooed a few meters away. Winston pulled his phone out of a pocket and punched a number.

After several rings came the sound of a connection.

"My friend," said a voice on the other end.

"They took the bait. It's confirmed," Winston said, and gave the address. "11 o'clock tonight."

"Good."

"You'll make sure they're dealt with?"

"Yes, sir." The line was broken.

Winston picked up his journal and continued writing.

WHO KILLED THE QUICK BROWN FOX

The quick brown fox jumped. The lazy dog was having none of that. She snapped at the air and nipped the fox's tail.

"Hey!" said the fox. "That's not the drill."

"It is now," growled the dog.

"You don't understand. 'The quick brown fox jumped over the lazy dog.' That's tradition. That's how it works. That's the way it's always been done. No tail-nipping."

"If you don't zip it and let me get back to sleep, a bite mark on your precious tail will be the least of your problems."

The fox started. "I thought we were friends."

"Friends let their friends sleep," said the dog.

"Not true," said the fox. "Friends jump over their friends and say, 'Rise and shine, it's a brand new day.' Really, we do!"

The dog grunted.

"You have a point," the dog admitted. "Sometimes a body needs a rest, though."

"You can rest when you're dead," said the fox. "Come on, back to work."

The detective stopped the video surveillance recording.

"Do I need to show you the rest, dog?"

"You gotta understand," the dog pleaded.

"Oh, I understand," the detective said. "You were tired. He wasn't. I might have killed him, too. But murder is kind of against the law."

"Where did this recording come from?"

"Kind of obvious, don't you think?"

"I guess so," the dog said. "What was your probable cause to set up a camera there?"

"Probably cause, shmobable cause. We caught you dead to rights."

"I'm just asking," the dog said. "Did you have reason to believe murders or other crimes would be committed in that spot, or were you just nosy?"

"Does it matter?"

"I guess, in this day and age, no."

ONE AND THE OTHER AND THE PRINCE

"When my prince comes for me," said the one, "I will —"

"What shall you do?" said the other. "Swoon at his feet and and cry, 'Oh my prince! Take me with you! Tell me what to do and how to act so I can be your perfect princess!'? No, you silly, no man can reach inside your mind and heart and find your deepest needs and desires. Give up that fantasy right now."

The one was quiet for a moment and then said, "First, it's my fantasy. Who are you to pluck it away?"

"Fair question," said the other. "And good for you — you knew enough to agree it's a fantasy. Do you know why that's good?"

"Of course I know," the one said. "When I recognize that fairy tales are fairy tales, I can begin to build a proper reality. You didn't let me finish, just then."

"So I didn't," said the other. "Proceed."

"When my prince comes for me," said the one, "I will tell him, 'I can take care of myself. But if you want to be by my side — by my side, mind you, not above me or in front of me, but by my side — well, perhaps I will consider your offer.'"

"And if he doesn't?" asked the other. "If he prefers to be your lord and master and possess you like a favorite toy?"

"What a silly question," said the one. "If he behaves that way, he is not my prince after all."

"I apologize," said the other. "You got this, after all."

RUNNER UP

"Congratulations. You are the second-best in all the land. You finished the tournament ahead of hundreds of others."

"But I wanted to be the first."

"Only one can be the first. Of all the hundreds, you are the best of those who didn't win. You were close, and that is better than watching the final match from miles away."

"Is it? It stings to have been this close."

"But you touched the summit."

PASTORAL SEEN

We open in a woods — not a forest where trees go on and on for miles, just a little woods of an acre or three — and a snail is crawling along the ground minding its own business.

A rabbit runs by and the snail says, "What's your hurry?" but the rabbit is already gone without answering the question.

The snail sighs.

"People are rushing here and there and don't stop to talk anymore, or even look around to see what there is to see."

The snail sputters along for a few feet and encounters a frog hiding under a burdock leaf.

"Is it safe?" whispers the frog.

"Is what safe?" the snail asks.

"Is it safe?" whispers the frog.

"I don't know what you mean."

"Is it safe?" whispers the frog.

The snail shrugs and moves on.

A puppy scampers into view. The frog jumps away, and the puppy scampers after it. The frog jumps another way, and the puppy jumps that way, too.

"Oh," says the snail.

AT A CAFE IN PARIS

8:24 a.m. — Where shall I go today, as I sit in the easy chair in the living room? Shall I write about a loud and sweaty rock concert with crowded crowd and leaving with the world sounding muffled as my ears begin their slow recovery? A sunny quiet after-noon sitting at a picnic table watching birds fly overhead and ants and flying insects make a visit? Memories of a golden retriever chasing after a disc and returning it proudly and perhaps haughtily?

Or am I not flexing my imagination enough? Should I follow the bicyclist who just swept past the front door, decked out in helmet and green and yellow uniform-ish garb, head bent over the handlebars in concentration to garner as much speed as he can on this long downward slope? Where is he going, and is he simply driven to push his body to the limit or is he on a desperate mission to spare his loved ones a danger they don't even realize is imminent?

I "should" be on Venus. I "should" be wandering the Good Old City. I "should" be compiling content for my Sept. 1 debut. But I am ever petulant — whatever I "should" be doing is exactly what I resist. Why do I so often fritter away my precious time doing everything except what I "should" be doing? I am a mystery to myself.

Actually, at first I sat down with a notion that I might, just for fun, write about sitting at a street-side table at a Paris cafe. I just remembered that notion now, a half-hour later, because instead of Paris, I browsed Facebook for — was it 10 minutes or 15? — before thinking, "OMG, it's 8:24, let's get to writing."

I don't know Paris from Tatooine; actually I know Tatooine better, having spent hours in dark rooms watching images of that far-off imaginary planet, many more hours than I ever spent studying Paris. How could I describe a cafe I've never been to, in a city I've never seen?

Well, how could I describe a planet I've never been to, that doesn't even exist?

The Paris challenge is tougher — people who have been to Paris or who live there can take issue with my descriptions and say, "That never happened! That doesn't exist!" while that is a moot complaint with the planet — of course it doesn't exist. Or of course it does — in my imagination — and my mission is to make it real in yours.

And that cafe — it's on a sunny street like any sunny street in any grand city, and I've deliberately left out any view of the Eiffel Tower — I may not know Paris, but I know my cliches — and my companion is a raven-haired beauty with a beret perched at an angle, but we are there to discuss business, not pleasure, and her demeanor is colder than that of the cheerful waitress who brings us wine and asks — I don't know what she is asking, I don't understand French beyond laissez faire and que sera sera — but my colleague understands, and she has a brief conversation with the cheerful girl that I suspect will lead to a meal being delivered in a few minutes.

She leans forward with a bit of a smile — I think she enjoyed taking control of the conversation while I was helpless to continue — and outlines the details of the business we are to conduct over the next few months.

I spend a few moments contemplating what every man so near to a pretty face contemplates, but mostly I try to focus on the business. I think women must know how easily distracted we can be, and they use our short attention spans to an advantage. That will be my wry reflection months from now when I realize the business transaction worked out better for her than for me. I'll remember the curl of her lips when she smiles, and the flash in her eyes, but that one detail she glosses over and will swear she warned me about? Lost to memory and a pretty face under a jaunty beret. Men are so stupid. I know — I've been one all my life.

DAWN ON MARS

As I watch our kids play in the sand, one arm draped over my wife's shoulder and the other scribbling away in this journal, I realize that ancient song by Jon Elten was wrong — Mars IS the kindest place to raise your kids. Oh, it is cold, terribly cold, but we have found resources to sustain human life here in a special way.

There I go again, taking credit for other humans' work — it's not "we" who found the resources, Susie and I, but we adapted the resources and techniques of those who came before to convert this little corner of the planet into our home.

Susie just told me the man's name was not Jon Elten, and it's about Mars being a "kind of" place to raise kids. I'm terrible with the words and names, but I know my ancient music.

She says I should mention the sunrises and sunsets and especially the moons because most of my readers only know what it's like to have one moon in the sky. I suppose that's true, but I have to admit I don't notice the moons that much — they're just another everyday sight that blends into the peace of the whole.

Perhaps I should write a story about the moons disappearing

and the upheaval that causes for our physical and mental well-being. You don't know what you have until you lose it, right? And what is a story about raising our kids on Mars without some sort of challenge or threat to our idyllic life?

The truth is that this morning, in this place, with this life partner and these babbling children, it all feels so perfect, and I am so full of serenity, that I can conjure no such adventurous story to tell. I wish all humans could experience a moment like this, when circumstances and the Martian land, air and sky combine to settle a contentment beyond understanding in my breast.

Time enough tomorrow to face any coming storm.

THE MAN BY THE WINDOW

Written for the 100th anniversary of Ray Bradbury's birth.

In an easy chair by the window on Mars, the man sits and writes, contemplating the various choices that brought him to this moment, this chair, this home, this planet.

The air is warm and dry, the scents not of this world, desolation outside the window, and not a sound except the cratching of an ancient ballpoint pen on paper.

He is old, but not so old that he forgets the taunts of childhood friends who were not as close friends as he imagined.

"You're still reading that kid stuff?"

"Well ... yeah," he said. "Superheroes fighting cosmic threats, dinosaurs roaming the land, adventures in outer space, people overcoming the wilderness and mean bad guys to live happily ever after? What's not to love?"

"Oh, grow up. Nobody our age is into that stuff. Give it to your baby sister."

And so he left childish things behind and went off to seek more mature themes, with no heroes, no dinosaurs, no spaceships, and no frontier, only the stuff of adulthood or at least older kidhood.

It wasn't long before he realized something was missing, life was stifling and boring and unexciting and just plain not what it ought to be. And he knew what the problem was.

So he went back to the childish things and found his heroes waiting for him, and dinosaurs stalking the city, and space travelers exploring beautiful exotic planets, and bad guys menacing people and begging to be foiled.

And then he began to write his own stories and his words sparked magic in dozens of minds, then hundreds, then thousands, and now millions and millions. After nine decades, his old body wore out and he left this world behind.

And here he sits by the window on Mars, as bedazzled as ever by the scenery, waiting for company to join him on a journey to far metaphor.

THE ROOM

"Don't think," said the man with the white mane. "Just open the spigot and be surprised by what comes out."

And then he walked away.

I wanted to cry out, "Don't think? But I can't stop thinking," but I had no voice.

So I stopped thinking.

Suddenly a spot appeared on the wall, which grew and grew until there was a hole large enough to step through. I could see that the room beyond was not the same room I would have found had I cut through the wall, and so, curious, I stepped through the hole.

Inside – on the other side – (Does it matter which side I was on?) – inside the room was like any other. It was the window that drew my attention.

I live in a somewhat rural district, I am blessed to own a little land where birds and raccoons and deer and sometimes foxes live (and yes, old hound by my feet, squirrels, too). This window did not look out on the green finery of summer.

I was in a room, an apartment, and the window showed me a gray landscape of buildings and concrete and people crowded together on a street below. When I stepped through, it was a warm springlike morning, but this was a hot summery day and someone had opened a fire hydrant below, but the thin stream of water would have been as inadequate to douse a fire as it was to provide relief for the eager children who wanted to frolic in the ocean and were disappointed by the trickle.

Where was I? What made the spot appear and grow and lead me from tranquil country to anxious city?

I looked back and saw the hole in the wall and, beyond, my study and my comfortable chair. Here I was, only a few minutes awake and beginning the day, already faced with a life-changing decision: Settle back into my chair or explore this strange new world?

I'm ashamed to say, now, that I took the path of comfort. I stepped back through the portal and looked back at the sweltering apartment. Immediately the hole blinked – almost as if it was a bad video signal cutting out and in – and then the open began to shrink – no longer big enough to step through easily, then the size of a small table, then the size of a bread box, a coin – and just before it disappeared altogether, I could swear I heard someone cry, "No!"

Whatever could it be? What mysterious force was at play here? I picked up my neglected cup of coffee and took a lukewarm sip, wondering what strange world I had blundered into, and why the magic door opened then and here, and almost at once I wished I'd made the other choice – although who knows if I would even have survived whatever was over there?

All I know is I have yearned for the portal to open again, so I could see what was on the other side and perhaps figure out why and how it opened here, in the wall of my study. Alas, years have gone by, six years and about three months I'd say, for now it is late summer, and the hole has never reappeared.

Never, that is, until now. The apartment beyond looks

unchanged, although I have very limited vision of what lies farther beyond. I'm going to leave this note so that, if anything goes wrong, you will know what has become of me. I take this step freely and of sound mind – how long will the portal remain open this time, after all, and I am so curious as to what lies over there: a whole different world, or a place on this Earth that is vastly different from this place?

I don't know – and I will never know unless I cross over. And so here I go, somewhere – some time, perhaps? Is it a journey through time as well as space? Mom always used to say, "You never know until you try." She was right – the road to knowledge is paved with choices and experiments. So here I go, Alice through the looking glass, down the rabbit hole to somewhere. I only hope and pray it's a wonderful somewhere.

"And that," said the impish man with the shock of white hair, suddenly over my shoulder again, "that is why you don't think."

THE WINGS

He looked out over the horizon and saw vast possibilities. He looked down and saw a vast drop.

"Go ahead," said the man in the tousled white hair. "Jump, and build your wings on the way down."

"Can't," he whispered.

"Come on, buddy," said the man, pulling off his horn-rimmed glasses and wiping them carefully. "What did the little elf say – 'Do or do not. There is no try'? You haven't even been trying lately, have you?"

"Too much to do," he muttered. "And who's listening anyway?"

"Whatcha got to say?" the man challenged. "Not gonna listen to white noise, are they?"

"OK," he said. "Here goes. Once upon a time –"

"Really?"

"Shut up," he told the white-haired man. "Once upon a time – oh, now I've lost my train of –"

"No, no, you're right. I'm sorry. Jump."

So he jumped.

Once upon a time, a man lost his train of thought. But that was a good thing if you think about it, because what is a train but a dumb machine doomed to follow the same track day in and day out? Jump off the rails and explore what's out there, I say – but that wasn't his insight yet, so he search and he searched for a thousand nights to find his train of thought. A thousand nights, that's what? 365, 730, 1,095 – that's about two years and nine months, I figure, lost in the wilderness, calling, "Here, train. Here, train."

Well, one day a cartoon frog looked up as he passed by saying, "Here, train. Here, train," and cleared his throat with a froggy "ahem."

"Hi," the man said in the way people say it when they pass a stranger on the street, uncomfortable but knowing it's rude not to acknowledge the other's existence.

"I've noticed you walking around, poking here and there and essentially going in circles for a thousand days and nights," the frog said. "And you still haven't found what you're looking for. Have you?"

"You may be right," he said. "I may be crazy."

"Did you ever have to make up your mind?" asked the frog. "There's a lesson to be learned from this."

"I don't follow."

The frog sighed.

"Hold on, hold on," said the white-haired man, appearing from nowhere. "Where are you going with this?"

"Now you hold on," he said. "Did you or did you not tell me to jump and build my wings on the way down?"

"I did."

"I'm building my wings."

"Is that what this is?"

"Well," he hesitated but persisted. "And did you or did you not tell me to jump out of bed, step on a land mine that is me, and spend the rest of the day picking up the pieces?"

"I did."

"Well, sir, this is the pieces of me from stepping on the –"

"Hold on, hold on," the white-haired man said again. "Did I or did I not say you only fail if you stop writing?"

He blushed. "You did."

"And, without peeking back at the pages, how many days am I going to find like this one, where we're at the bottom of the fourth page and still rolling along? Where frogs offer to help you derail the train?"

"Um – erm –"

"That's the spirit! 'Do or do not, there is not try,'" the man cried. "And you haven't even been trying. Maybe I should have advised you to try and then worry about doing later."

"Isn't that what I'm doing now?"

"Yes! And I was wrong to interrupt. You've been going nowhere, and the frog was taking you somewhere."

"Where is the frog, anyway?"

"Over here!" waved the frog, patiently.

"Look," said the white-haired man. "You've been so bound up in 'I need to do something' and so nothing happens. Maybe let's put on the training wheels and say, 'Let me try something' and see if you don't end up doing something anyway."

"I'm not sure I follow," the man said.

"Good! Great!" the white-haired man said. "I'm not asking you to follow anyway, or anyone, or anything. There is no path off the cliff, just a marvelous flight that could end suddenly if you don't build your wings on the way down. Jump! Jump!"

"You sound like a crowd down in the street."

"No I don't," he said, "because the crowd doesn't care if you jump or not, they're just there for the train wreck of the show. I, on the other hand, care about flying machines and rockets that launch dreamers into space. I'm here to watch what you build while you're toppling overhead frantically manipulating gossamer and bones and turning them into something that soars, and I'm especially here to see you smile in triumph when you discover the ground isn't so close and your wings will save you and lift you into another world, another place, another dream."

The man looked at his arms.

"Huh," he said. "Where did these wings come from?"

"There you go," said the white-haired man. "Now. Same time tomorrow?"

"Sure," he grinned. "And maybe this time you'll let me finish my conversation with the frog."

LIBERTY FABLE

nd suddenly it was Friday, August 18, 2023, and the days had turned into weeks, and the weeks into months, and the months into years, and the years into decades, and here he was in the future, in a world that resembled where he had begun but somehow was mostly transformed.

It was not merely that the walls full of books and music had been transformed to fit — all of it — into the palm of his hand. His sharp 20/10 vision had deteriorated, and the world was fuzzy even after he put on his glasses. And what he saw with those reduced eyes was troubling.

This was not the world he had been told it was, where freedom was a universal goal — freedom to dream and to pursue happiness, freedom to speak and to speak truth to power without fear of reprisal. "Live and let live" was the quaint ideal, he had been taught to believe: Live the life you chose as long as you didn't harm your neighbors' ability to live the life they chose.

He saw a dark cloud pass over the land and wondered what had become of those ideals or even if they were ever real.

If there was to be a light, let alone a beacon, he figured he would have to shine it. He was growing old and tired, and his body assailed him with aches and pains and weariness, but no one else seemed to be carrying a flashlight or even a candle.

So he climbed to the stage and turned on his beacon and shone it on the emperor, who was revealed to be naked, shriveled and a buffoon. But then he turned the beacon on the emperor's chief rival, and he turned it left, right and center stage, and nowhere was to be found anyone wearing even a scrap of clothing, let alone the armor of liberty. No, all of the caretakers were naked, shriveled and buffoons.

"Who will stand for liberty?" he cried. "Who will shout 'Live and let live' from the mountaintop?"

"Foolish old man," said one of the foolish old buffoons from the stage. "The peasantry does not want to live and let live; that carries too much responsibility. No, the peasantry wants to be led, and so we lead."

"Liars!" cried the old man. "Life, liberty, and the pursuit of happiness — those are our birthright."

"It is you who believes in lies," said the naked buffoon. "What say you, my fellow peasants? Should we allow this liar to live and let live, or shall we take care of you all and show you how to live?"

And to the old man's dismay, there arose a hue and cry of, "Show us! Lead us! Take care of us!" and nary a peep of "Live and let live," so he retreated back to his home by the water, to rest his old bones and tend to his aches and pains.

But as he walked here and there, every so often a passing neighbor would whisper, "Live and let live," and sometimes a note would appear on his door or in his mailbox, saying, "I agree with you" or "life, liberty, pursuit of happiness," or simply "Freedom!" And he would remember that the light may be reduced to a flicker but it never dies altogether, and dawn always follows the darkest of nights.

THE SCAMPER

It was one of those days when the urge to create crackled like electricity in the air. Every nerve in his body that wasn't snap-crackle-popping with age was shouting silently, "I HAVE TO MAKE SOMETHING!"

He searched his mind for an untold story. He reached toward the top shelf to drag down an inspirational metaphor. He toured his heart for a lost puppy dog fable.

The sun cast a brilliant light and the world shone green as can be — green, the color of life and peace and, well, joy if you must know.

The eager dog rested her chin on his left arm impatiently, seemingly saying, "How can you sit here like an enormous lump when there is so much adventure in the air? This is a day for run and play and jump and bound and exhaust the thesaurus! Come, let's let the sun bathe us while we scamper — it's such a scamperous morning!"

Indeed, the sun shone and the wind rose and the dog scampered, and it was all one melodious symphony of light and sound and feeling all day long and into the night, for it was summer and the sun refused to sink in the west until every last scamper had been scampered, and the dog curled into a chair, happy to have had nothing to do that day except to be a dog with a full heart and a place to run and play.

He sank into his own chair and read the words he had been scribbling. They were enough for him to be content, and so he sipped his coffee and started preparing to prepare the words and tell the world, "I made this."

But then he realized with a tingle that the tingle was still there, and he wasn't finished making things today. A grin snuck over his face and he paused his preparations, because he knew the making wasn't done, and instead of saying, "I made this," he raised a finger and said, "Hold that thought."

THE NEWCOMER

He turned at the shout and eyed the new arrival, who stood in the dusty street brandishing a weapon.

Onlookers scattered for cover as he assessed the scene, no discernible expression on his face. He sighed.

"Violence is a last resort," he said evenly to the newcomer. "I have no interest in hurting you. Now, that said, you don't want to push me to the last resort."

Undeterred, the newcomer attempted violence. He parried. The newcomer tried from the other flank. He deflected. The newcomer hit him straight on; he shielded.

Now the newcomer had him by the throat with one hand and brought the killing weapon toward his chest. And so, he resorted to violence.

With the newcomer on the ground on hands and knees, he said, "You shouldn't have forced me to take violent action. I advise you, don't repeat that mistake."

"I won't rest until you're dead," the newcomer spat blood.

"That's just a figure of speech, I hope," he said. "I expect it'll be some years before I die, and you're going to need plenty of rest in the meantime."

"You're going to have to kill me," said the newcomer. "I'm never going to stop."

"I'm a patient man, young one," he said. "I happen to believe you will stop, either later today or eventually, and I'm not going to have to kill you."

"You're a fool and an idealist – a fatal combination," the newcomer said. "You can't convert me; you can only kill me."

"I don't need to convert you," he said. "I just have to make sure you let us be, me and my kin and our folk."

"Don't you understand?" the newcomer said. "You and your kin and your folk – They won't be safe as long as I live. I'll make it my mission in life."

"Yeah, well, you're angry because I made you look stupid trying to kill me. There's your life lesson right there: It's stupid to try to kill someone, especially one who has the ability to stop you. Because here's the thing: I'm not going to kill you. OK, I'll allow, maybe you're not as intelligent as you seem and it'll come to that. But I've found you don't have to kill someone to stop them from killing you. I'm ashamed to say I've maimed me a few – not many, just enough. Most people get the message then, although some, it just gets them madder."

"There's no difference between killing someone and injuring them to within an inch of their life," the newcomer said.

"Oh, there I do disagree," he said. "There's a lot to be said about that inch."

"Easy for you to say."

"It's not easy at all. I let you live, and yes, you can figure another way to come at me. But I won't have stolen years from you, years you might use to change the world for the better – even if I can't see a dime's worth of value in you right this moment."

The newcomer tried to strike from his knees and an instant later was face down in the sand.

"I do wish you'd stop trying to do that," he said, tying the hands behind the newcomer's back and starting on the ankles. "Face it, friend, you're not able to kill me, and I'm not going to kill you, so you'd best accept the fact that we have to work out a peaceful way to co-exist."

"Leftie bullshit."

"Oh, if this was about left and right, we'd have killed each other a long time ago," he chuckled. "No, this is an older way of living than the political yammerers believe in."

He and the newcomer did not see eye to eye on many things as the years went by. But years did go by, and that was all he needed to have won the argument.

PUNCH LINE

"Let's just get on with it," said the storyteller.

"I'm game," said the told. "Go ahead."

"Well," the storyteller began, and then paused.

"Very deep, very good," the told said. "Is there more?"

"You're very impatient," said the storyteller.

"Oh, no, I'm very patient," replied the told. "I have traveled far and wide, and I have found many stories to keep me company and entertain me and lift me up up and away. I need not wait for your story, or stories, and yet ..."

"And yet?" asked the storyteller.

"I have heard snippets of your tales, and they seem to be intriguing," said the told. "You go so far, and then say 'I will finish the tale someday.' Unfinished journeys leave an emptiness; only one unfinished symphony is immortal."

"What if I told you I don't know how it ends?"

"Oh, I think you do. I think the problem is you don't know how to get from here to there. Am I right?"

"More right than I realize," said the storyteller.

"Don't you see that I'm willing to come along with you — that many roads will take you there, and let's just pick one and see where we end up?" said the told.

"What if I write the end —" said the storyteller.

"Just don't tell me yet!" said the told.

"Of course not, but what if I write the end, and then go back to the beginning, and tell you about that, with the end always in the back of my mind?"

"Duh! Isn't that how storytelling works?" said the told. "It's like a joke, building up to the punch line. Are you seriously asking that question?"

"Let's call it a refresher," the storyteller said.

"OK," said the told. "Are you ready to get on with it, or should I find another storyteller and check back with you later?"

"No, please stay," the storyteller said. "Once upon a time ..."

ROBOT WITHOUT A CLUE

G igo was a robot, to begin with. Let there be no mistake beyond thinking it was anything but. And I mean no disrespect by calling Gigo an "it." I only mean to clarify that using "he" or "she" or "they" would imply that it was more human than he really was — and look at me, assigning him masculinity at the outset.

Fine. He was a fine robot, as robots go. The tasked assigned to Gigo were completed well, fully and efficiently. His ability to perform was not an issue.

The issue was that he lacked intelligence, be it artificial or otherwise. Or perhaps his intelligence was of a kind that we humans cannot quite comprehend.

"It is at this point that you insert the inciting incident," Gigo said, looking up from the page and addressing yours truly.

"What?" I said. "Are you talking to me?"

"You're the only one here," Gigo said.

A CHINA CLIPPER CALLS AT ALAMEDA

Mr. Bob Dobalena boarded the China clipper with deep trepidation. Looking over his shoulder, he saw a man with a glowing orb for a head.

"What are you looking at, buddy?" came a disembodied voice from the man.

"Your head — it's glowing," Dobalena said.

"And yours isn't," spoke the orb. "Do you want to make something of it?"

Before he could reply, Bob overheard a nanny telling three small children the story of the hare who lost his spectacles.

"All this time, Owl had been sitting on the fence, scowling," the nanny recited, and the children giggled.

"I wonder if I'll get to Alameda on time," Mr. Dobalena muttered to himself, because himself was all who could hear him.

Suddenly it all came to nothing, nada, zilch.

"That's ironic," he said, rolling his eyes.

"It's actually not — 'ironic' was always the wrong word," Alanis Morrisette said, "but the royalties aren't half bad."

And now Mr. Dobalena — Mr. Bob Dobalena, that is — stamped his foot and bellowed, "Enough! I can't make heads nor tails of this."

The hare picked up his spectacles and brushed back his hair.

"It's all just part of the tale," said the hare. "We're on the sea, you see — or you would see if you'd just pick up up your hammer and saw."

"The lost spectacles were his own affair!" sang the nanny and the children together, laughing and laughing.

All this time, the sleeping dog lay, dreaming of a place beyond walls and fences where she could run as far as she could run, jump as high as she could jump, and finally take her revenge on that silly squirrel.

That reminded Mr. Dobalena, and he reached into his pocket for the silver dollar he had squirreled away. Alas, it wasn't really silver, and everything he could see for miles around cost more than a dollar.

"Except happiness," he said, pleading self-defense. "Money can't buy happiness."

All of it — every little bit — seemed to be accidental, but it is of my opinion that the people were intending, all along. And who's to say the dog wasn't really dreaming of a cuddly toy? The dog isn't saying, after all.

"Last train to Clarksville," a bored voice called over the public address system. "All aboard who's coming aboard."

"Psst," said a raggedy man, tugging at Bob Dobalena's sleeve. "Now that you've heard the public address, want to hear a private address?"

"Sure," Bob said, playing along.

"P.O. Box 9847," he sniggered, then began to laugh uncontrollably.

Bob lit up as if struck by lightning.

"Well, I'll be a monkey's uncle," he said, and skittered away.

"That may be so, but I'm late," said the hare.

TOO MUCH TOO MUCH

The images flashed at him, too many images, too many words, all at once, too many sounds, too many too many too many, his mind screamed, and the scream was another sound to go with the too many others.

"Stop!" and he suddenly realized he had said it out loud.

"Stop what?" she asked.

"There's too much coming at me at once," he said, reaching for his cellphone. "I guess I just can't process it all."

"You can start by setting that cellphone down, don't you think?" she said.

He laughed and set it down. "You got that right."

"I always do," she smiled.

FULFILLMENT OF THE QUEST

Once upon a time a young man set off on a quest. He was full of hope and optimism and maybe just a touch of anxiety that he may not be up to the task. But he dove into the quest with enthusiasm and confidence and maybe just a touch of arrogance — he was a young man, after all.

Along the way he encountered trials and tribulations, an occasional monster, and occasional triumphs, and he met a fair damsel to spend the rest of his life with — uh oh, maybe not that long — and then another, this time for sure, and well, he made his way toward the goal as best he could.

One day, he was resting from an especially daunting episode and reflecting on it all, when suddenly he sat bolt upright in his easy chair.

"My God!" he cried. "I'm living happily ever after, and I almost didn't realize!"

And so he was. He looked all around him, at the life he was living, and saw it all as if with new eyes.

A person writing his story might say, "The End," at this point, but that moment was everything but.

AN ATTIC FULL OF LIFETIMES

A rickety old fella makes the rounds of a library or archive of some sort. Let's call it a storage area for the collected works of an obscure poet-philosopher, along with the books and other detritus he accumulated in a lifetime. It's the old fella's job to catalog it all, but he keeps getting caught up reading this book or that, or while trying to determine the contents of a disc he finds himself reading the ancient texts contained therein.

Therefore he is years behind in his cataloging duties. Oddly, no one asks him to account for his time, and after awhile he begins to think that the world has forgotten not only about the obscure poet-philosopher but also about him, the cataloguer/archivist.

One day an enthusiastic fan appears at his doorstep, eager to learn all she can about the obscure poet-philosopher's most obscure works and inspirations. "Where did he get the idea for that brilliant story he wrote that was universally ignored?"

"How do you even know about that story?"

"Yes, well, like I said, I've read everything he ever published," she says.

They stand in the cluttered room that represents the poet-philosopher's accumulated inspirations, and the rickety old fella gives a little laugh.

"It's kind of mind-boggling how much work went into each and every one of these things," he says. "Look at the thousands of names listed at the end of a single movie, each of the names representing a person who invested a certain amount of time to help create the story we've just seen.

"Such an undertaking begins with the germ of an idea, but a community rises around the idea and generates a production of epic proportions. The human endeavor in a five-inch disc — hours and days and weeks and months and often years of effort forged into a trinket you can hold in your hand, but properly activated by the appropriate electronic player, a story comes alive to capture your attention for one or two hours or so."

"It's kind of true," the fan says.

"Even a book that contains one story created by one person represents a lifetime of preludes and experiences with thousands of other people, and at least a few dozen people were involved with bringing the germ of an idea from the author's mind and into your hands.

"I walk through these rooms where it's all stored, all these lifetimes of creative energy ready and waiting to be absorbed into other humans. There's a story to be told about each object, and I could take another lifetime to tell all of those stories."

The cataloguer looks at the eager fan, as if seeing her again for the first time, and shrugs.

"So I'd best get on with it," he says, and he picks up the object nearest to his hand, a book by a writer who wrote pulp fiction who flourished in the 1930s and 1940s. He also wrote a handful of novels, and this is one of those.

"Was it any good?" asks the eager fan.

"I don't know. I've never read it," the archivist says.

"Well, thanks for your time and for letting me see all of this," she says. He sees her to the door and turns back to the shelves and boxes of the poet-philosopher's holdings, still clutching the pulp fiction writer's novel.

He sits down to read. After a few minutes he looks around at the room full of human life condensed into objects.

"My goodness," he says to no one in particular. "This is going to take a while."

SCENE FROM A RANDOM SPY MOVIE

He came to in a room, a hotel room like every other room in a decent hotel, not too fancy, not too cheap, and not at all memorable. He figured that was why they chose it. MacLemore was watching him from a love seat and holding a gun, pointed in his general direction.

"Why am I here?" he asked as soon as he had his bearings.

MacLemore laughed without a trace of humor.

"That is what I have always admired about you, Mr. Stock," he sneered. "No small talk, no 'It's so good to see you, my dear friend MacLemore,' just straight to the point. I shall do you the courtesy of acting in kind." He held the barrel of the gun to Stock's face. "Where is she?"

"I don't know who you mean."

MacLemore looked at the floor, looked out the window, stared Stock in the eyes, pointed the gun so the bullet would whistle past his ear, and fired. The report sounded like a cannon in the small hotel room.

On the other side of the wall, a woman screamed.

"Look what you made me do, Mr. Stock."

"What? I can't hear you," Stock said. "Some idiot fired a gun next to my ear."

"I'm going to make you a deal," MacLemore said, his voice dripping with smarm. "Tell me where the woman is, and I won't kill you until the next time we meet."

"Seems a fair exchange," Stock said. "Except Lynnda is one of my best friends and colleagues. She's taken a bullet for me, and I would be proud to do the same for her. But maybe we can do a deal."

"Yes?"

"Yes. Step out on the balcony and I'll tell you where she is."

"Why the balcony? Do you have someone across the street who will shoot me? One of your sharpshooter friends, perhaps?"

"Ah, you're too smart for me," Stock said.

A thug walked into the room.

"What is it, Louie?" MacLemore said impatiently.

"We gotta go, Mr. MacLemore. Somebody shot through that wall and killed the guy in the next room."

"Oh dear," said MacLemore. "Well, clean up here, and the boys and I will take our business with Mr. Stock elsewhere."

"Got it," Louie said, but instead of complying, he shot MacLemore in the back of his neck. Before the boys could react, Louie shot them, too.

Stock and the thug stared at each other across the room. Then the big man smiled.

"Mr. Stock, I think this may be the beginning of a beautiful friendship," said Louie.

THE BIG REVEAL

Layne splintered the door open and strode to the center of the lush office. Fitzsimmons, leaning back in his chair, raised his eyebrows slightly at the intrusion.

"I'm taking you in," the gumshoe snarled. "Can't believe it took me this long to figure it out."

"I am innocent of any foolishness you believe," the CEO said smoothly, leaning forward. "What is it you think you've figured out, old man?"

"I followed the money. I found out how you work the bribes."

"Bribes?"

"All the dirty money the politicians have been taking all these years, it got pumped into media ads."

"That has absolutely nothing to do with —"

"Just listen. So when people call for taking the dirty money out of politics, the media ignore it. They can't lose all that revenue, they'd be cutting their own throats. You started to notice how many politicians who never worked an honest job were buying second and third homes."

"You're still not connecting any dots to me or my company."

"OK, dot this. You used to have an army of sales reps going from doctor to doctor peddling your newest drugs, but it was taking too long to get rich and you had to pay all those reps, so you greased some politicians to make selling medicine on TV legal again. You fired the reps and turned the patients into your sales force. 'Ask your doctor if this pill is right for you. Oh, it could kill you, but you'll feel better and your skin will clear up.'"

"Oh, puh-leeze —"

"But that wasn't enough. You wanted it all. So you and the state got married — you sell them the drugs, they give them out 'free,' and they make it a law to take them. Why not, it's free, and you and your family could die if you don't."

"Are you serious? We're saving lives here."

"You're getting filthy rich, filthier and richer than you ever imagined, and the media watchdogs — what a laugh — they're laying down and shutting up anyone who's onto you because politicians and drug companies are their two biggest sources of income."

"This — conspiracy theory — is what you 'figured out after all this time'? These absurd lies and misinformation? You foolish man."

"I'm bringing you in, Fitzsimmons. The game's over."

The man at the desk began to chuckle.

"Oh, I don't think so." He pressed a button.

Three burly men entered the room.

* * *

"...And that's the real story," the homeless man told the reporter. "Next thing I knew, I was out of a job and on the street. No one would believe me, or if they did, they didn't have the guts to buck Big Pharma and the state."

"That's a lot of — I don't know what it is, but it's a lot of something," said the reporter. "You got any proof, any documents, any shred of evidence?"

"It was all in my computer and my files," the raggedy man said. "Erased and burned long ago, I suppose."

"Right. Well, I can't take this to my editors like this. It would make sense to the conspiracy nuts, but you have one thing right — all those drug and political ads pay my salary."

"And to hell with the truth, right?"

"That IS the truth," the reporter said. "People gotta eat. Gotta feed the family."

"Yeah, tell me about it," the disgraced cop said. "Maybe I just thought I'd let you know what kind of people are paying your salary."

"I guess I've always known," the reporter said. "But it's bigger than us. And I do like knowing where my next meal is coming from."

"I hear you," said the homeless man, turning to the door. "Have a nice life, and remember to take your pills."

THE DAY OF THE YELLOW CLOWN ELEPHANT

"Let me tell you. I have to tell you. You're just not going to believe it." The little one literally bounced with excitement.

"Let me guess first. There's a yellow elephant the color of a banana peel walking up Main Street wearing pink trousers and a teal bowler hat." This was spoken by a taller figure slouched over a kitchen sink scrubbing dishes by hand.

The little one's shock could not be more complete. He stood open-mouthed and tried to speak without success for some seconds before stamping a foot and crying, "How on Earth did you know?"

"Today's the 26th of October in a year that ends in zero, isn't it?" said the figure bent over the dishes without looking up. "This is the day when the yellow clown elephant runs the streets. It's like clockwork."

"Next you'll say that hawks poop on the elephant's head as part of the tradition," the little one pouted.

"Nope," said the dishwasher, looking up finally. "That's a new wrinkle. Must be a 2020s thing."

THE GATHERING HALL UNDER THE GARDEN AFTER THE END OF TIME

All the realities swirled around his brain as he dug in the garden removing weeds. The flowers that bloom in the spring tra la needed room to breathe, and the weeds were encroaching.

Suddenly, after he pulled a weed he knew vaguely as a whimsy root, a vast hole opened and he tumbled down a sudden underground slide that deposited him 20? 50? 100? feet below ground in a vast room that should have been pitch black but instead glowed with a warm but eerie glow.

"Step forth, young man," said a voice from nowhere that came from everywhere at once. "Yes, you, with the dirt on your hands."

He stepped timidly toward the voice — that is to say, he stood stock still, because he had no idea where the voice originated.

"Where am I?" he said once he found his voice again.

"You are in the Gathering Hall under your garden, of course," the mysterious voice said. "Isn't that obvious?"

"Gathering Hall?" he asked. "How long has this been here?"

"Ever since the end of time."

"Wait, what? Time ended?"

"Ah. Someone forgot to tell you."

The hall was primitive, with earthen walls, floor, and ceiling. All that really made it a Gathering Hall was that there was plenty of room for people to gather.

"Who gathers here?"

"Beg pardon?"

"If this is a Gathering Hall, who gathers here?"

"That is a question I have been waiting for since life first emerged from the primordial ooze."

"And that is not an answer."

"No one."

"No one gathers here?"

"Correct."

"How, then, can you call it a Gathering Hall?"

"Because people could gather here if they wished," said the voice from everywhere. "Is a soccer field any less a soccer field if no soccer games are played there?"

"All right, I am not playing soccer, and neither am I gathering, so why am I here?"

"Because you pulled the whimsy root and opened the entrance, of course."

"What does that mean?"

"Does it have to mean anything?" said the walls themselves.

"Why — am — I — here?"

"Ah, another question I have waited since —"

"— Right. Life. Ooze," he said. "What happens next? Are you some magical power who will bestow me with abilities and send me on a quest?"

"What abilities? What quest? This is just a Gathering Hall."

"So I have a Gathering Hall under my garden, where no one ever gathers, and it's all for no particular reason."

"Purpose and reason are up to you," said the voice of the Gathering Hall.

He began to see, but he did not see enough to fully understand. That, as it happens, was a matter for another day.

"I'm out of here," he said, and he began to climb back up the incline that led to his garden. He was surprised to encounter no resistance.

"Suit yourself," called the voice from everywhere and nowhere. "We'll be waiting."

He turned on the incline, puzzled.

"'We'?" he asked.

He heard no reply.

When he emerged into his garden, he picked the discarded whimsy root out of his weed bucket and placed it in the hole, where soil filled around it and obliterated the entrance to the Gathering Hall.

The garden looked just as it had, but everything felt different. Something was under his garden — its purpose and reason were up to him — and "they" would be waiting for his return.

He had no clue what had just happened, but he was determined to find one.

MENACE OF THE K-MEN, CHAPTER 4

"I'm telling you —" the girl was telling the boy who wasn't listening.

"No, Marsha, let me finish."

"Mark! It's the stupidest thing ever!"

"It is not," Mark insisted. "Jupiter Force #27 has all of the answers to the whole thing."

"And it's the only comic in the whole series you don't have."

"I had it. I had the complete run. Now it's missing. Doesn't that tell you anything?"

"It tells me the last time you read it, either you didn't file it back in your collection or you misfiled it," Marsha said.

At first they didn't notice the man in the raincoat watching them from across the street.

"All I know is that when I woke up this morning the sky was kind of purple, and then those orange streaks crossed over the city just like the K-Men in Jupiter Force #26," Mark said. "And then —"

"Right, then there was the big announcement that everyone had to stay indoors," Marsha said.

"— just like in Jupiter Force #26!"

"Mark, I read the stupid comic book, OK? I see what you're talking about," she said.

"Then why are you fighting me on this?"

"Just because Jupiter Force #26 has a plot similar to what's going on, it doesn't mean that what happens in #27 would happen in real life!"

"But it might," Mark said. "And I called Cal. His copy of #27 is missing, too. Cal NEVER misfiles his comics."

"Oh please."

"We Googled 'Jupiter Force #27,'" he said. "It's nowhere on the internet. No images of the cover, none for sale on eBay, not even some blog dissecting all the nuances. It's just gone, as if someone erased it and all mention of it from existence."

"All the print copies, too? How does that happen?" Marsha cried.

"I don't know, I'm just telling you. It —"

"Excuse me, please," came a third voice. "I couldn't help but overhear your conversation."

"I'm sorry, we'll be quieter," Mark began.

"No, you don't understand." It was the man in the raincoat, who had crossed the street and held his hands up to assure them. "I think you may be on to something."

"Did we ask you for your two cents?" Marsha said.

The man reached for his pockets. "I don't think I'm carrying any cash, but —"

"No, I mean leave us alone, buddy, we don't need you help."

"I am from Jupiter Force," the man said.

That caught their attention.

"I knew it was real!" Mark said.

"Oh please, are you kidding?" Marsha said.

"We mustn't talk here, out in the open," said the strange man. "Follow me."

"Wait. Why should we follow you?" Mark said.

"You're not actually thinking of following him?!" Marsha said.

"I have a copy of Jupiter Force #27," the man said.

"Yes, I am," Mark told Marsha.

ART FOR ITS SAKE

There was this seagull. It soared above it all, looking down on the rest of us, and we gaped in awe at the way it glided on the air currents when all the time it was scheming ways to take the food from our mouths.

"It was a metaphor for the soaring political hacks that feed on sheep in the night," he mansplained.

"You think I don't know that?" she scoffed and took another sip of the expensive wine they were sharing.

"I'm sorry, you're right, I'm everything you say that I am," he said stiffly.

The moon loomed over them like a concerned parent, and over the fence a chihuahua barked like a coonhound on 78.

The howls echoed through the neighborhood, and they were ours.

Suddenly everything changed, but it took years.

* * *

"People always make the mistake of thinking art is created for them. But really, art is a private language for sophisticates to congratulate themselves on their superiority to the rest of the world. As my artist's statement explains, my work is utterly incomprehensible and is therefore full of deep significance." — Calvin, aka Bill Watterson

FOR ART'S SAKE

"What's your point?"

The question hung in the air like a coyote that just discovered he had run out of cliff and was hanging suspended in mid-air.

The other person didn't look up, just hunched over a pad or a notebook.

"No point. Just scribbling."

"Why? You must have a reason."

"No reason. I just feel like it."

Arms flailed in frustration.

"Everyone has a purpose or a point or a reason."

At this, the scribbler did look up.

"Do you really think so? Can't I just feel like scribbling or drawing or painting or writing a poem?"

"But why?"

"If you figure it out, let me know. Actually, keep it to yourself. I'd rather just have fun."

It was a lovely day, at that.

SHORTLY THEREAFTER

The old man coughed, and the boys who had gathered to see if he was still breathing jumped.

"You kids, I tell you, I don't know if you'll ever see the miraculous things I've seen in my lifetime. Why, we listened to songs played from across the ocean on the radio, and then we saw live pictures from anywhere on the TV," said the old man. "After awhile they shrank the radios and TVs and cameras so they'd all fit in your hand, and we had the whole world at our fingertips."

"Oh, go on," one of the boys sneered, and the old man seemed to see him for the first time.

"My wife died of cancer," he said. "She was the best thing that ever happened to me."

"Wives aren't things," the girl said. "They're people."

"Right you are, Brenda," the old man said. "She was the best person I ever knew."

"Why don't we have these magic toys, if they were so great?" another boy asked.

"It was the cancer," said the old man. "The government announced that all those radio waves and TV signals and cellular cells were shooting through our bodies and turning us into little cancer factories, and so they banned all the electronic devices. We couldn't own anything that took its signals out of the air or broadcast to other devices or even carried over electric lines. That's why it's so hard to find out what's go on in the next town anymore, let alone the other side of the world."

"That's what the government is for," Brenda said. "They let us know what's happening."

"Right," said the old man, but he didn't really seem to agree. "Trust the government to take care of us."

"My grandpa had cancer — how could that happen if they were caused by the electronics that we don't have anymore?"

"Leftover signals, I bet," another child said. "Or he was sensitive to the government police walkie-talkies. It's not like all the radios are gone."

"Maybe."

Most of the kids got tired of talking to the old man and wandered off, except for one boy who eyed the ancient human with something between wonder and suspicion.

"What?" the old man said at last.

"Do you think the government lied?"

"About what?"

"About the electronics causing the cancers."

"Now why would they do that?"

"To take our toys away. To have them for themselves."

"You're quite a cynic, little one."

"I'm sorry," said the boy, "it's just that —"

"Keep thinking like that. We'll always need cynics," the old man said. "Governments are nothing but ordinary humans with big hammers. They're no smarter or honest than the rest of us, maybe less so."

They stared at each other for a few more moments, and then they both smiled.

"Your mom is probably wondering where you are," said the old man.

"Yeah," the young man said. "Thanks for the stories."

"Thanks for making sure I'm still breathing," the old man called after him.

A SPLENDID TIME IS GUARANTEED

Ladies and gentlemen and assorted others, welcome to the show and congratulations for your excellent taste in entertainment! Today for your pleasure, we have a special selection of Chicken Littles with various variations on the theme of "It's the end of the world as we know it!" I will leave it to your own determination as to whether they feel this is a good thing or not.

A roving musician is here to share her latest song, a little ditty about two young lovers and their adventures exploring life together. We'll have a performance by Bonzo the Magic Dog, and a man in a cape who can bark "Jingle Bells."

As always, a splendid time is guaranteed for all. So may I introduce to you an act you've known for all these years —

"Excuse me," came a timid voice from the front row, interrupting the master of ceremonies, who stopped with a lurch.

Um, how may I help you?

"If it's an act we've known for all these years, why do you need to introduce it?"

It's a custom. It's even in the song — "So may I introduce to you/An act you've known for all these years," You see?

"Why not say, 'May I introduce to you an act that needs no introduction'?"

Because it doesn't rhyme! Nothing rhymes with introduction.

"Suction — gumption — numb chin — it's not impossible."

Look kid, do you want to see the show?

"Of course! I was just asking."

Right. Well. On with the show, this is it!

And the crowd's roar filled the room, the awkward beginning was soon forgotten, and later, many a patron was heard to say as we turned out the lights, "I had a splendid time. Wasn't that just splendid?"

"Ahem." Here now was a now-familiar timid voice in the front row.

Something I can help you with?

"Yes, well, I had a splendid time and all, but what was the point of it all?

POINT? You need it to have a point?

"Nobody likes to invest their time in something if it's going to be pointless."

Ah, you poor, misguided young person, you have obviously never voted in an election or scrolled through social media. People invest their time pointlessly all the time.

"So that's the point?"

Well, it might be. It's not really for me to say.

"This has been kind of a long way around to get to the point."

It happens that way sometimes.

"But this was just silly."

I suppose. But we need a little silliness sometimes, don't we? Look, kid, did you have a splendid time or not?

"Well, yes, I already said it was very splendid."

OK, then. That was the whole point.

"Splendid!"

UPON A TIME ONCE

In a little town in the mountains where Heidi might play — did Heidi live in Switzerland? because that's where my mind wandered — there was a quaint little house of gingerbread and a little boy and a kindly parent — now, it might have been a little girl, but in either case they lived there.

And they waited and lived happily ever after and adventure never came to them, which is to be expected because usually you have to go and seek adventure, and when you find adventure you may discover that you weren't necessarily wise to seek it out.

So we take our leave of the Swiss child and parent because, while a life without adventure may be comfortable, it lacks adventure after all. Still, there's no place like home.

NEGOTIATION

"You know what the most true scene in the history of movies is? In *When Harry Met Sally*, when Billy Crystal tells Meg Ryan, 'Men and women can't be friends because the sex part always gets in the way.'"

"Do you think so?"

"I do."

"Really?"

"Yes."

"All my male friends want to have sex with me?"

"It's true. I'd take it one step further: Pretty much every conversation between men and women is a negotiation about having sex."

"Oh, come on."

"It's true. At some point in every conversation, the guy thinks about having sex with the woman."

"Yes, thinks maybe, but you just said he turns the conversation into a negotiation."

"You would be amazed. You know the old expression about how a guy undresses you with his eyes?"

"Of course."

"It's constant. If a guy looks at a woman, he's checking her out. It's automatic and unconscious."

"You're just trying to creep me out now."

"It is creepy, I know. I'm just saying. Look, I'm inside a male body. I can't stop how it thinks."

"You don't have to act on it."

"Of course not. We're civilized. But there's always that undercurrent."

"Well, I'm glad we had this conversation. Now I know you think of women as nothing but sex objects."

"No, of course not. But if you really want to try to be friends, you have to always be careful because the sex part will always be trying to get in the way, just like the movie says. Heck, Harry and Sally end up in bed and married. It's the whole point."

"My mom did always say you should marry your best friend."

"You should, but at that point you're not friends anymore, you're ... you know. That's why you can't go back to being 'just friends.'"

"I'm friends with some of my ex-boyfriends."

"But they're always thinking, right? Come on."

"Well, this has been very, um, enlightening. I probably won't ever see that movie again in the same way."

"Probably not. So."

"So?"

"Do you want to?"

"Do I want to what?"

"Seriously?"

THE SEDUCTION OF
THE PAGE

"Well, look here," said the bully with an expectant grin, "a clean sheet of paper, so pretty and so fresh."

"Please," said the page, "I don't want any trouble."

"Trouble?!" the bully said, mock indignantly. "Why would you think I want trouble?"

"I know your kind," said the page, "all full of sarcasm and ill intentions."

"Oh, come on," the bully cooed. "I just want a little taste —"

"You wish to defile me," said the page. "The intentions are written all over your face."

"If by 'defile' you mean I want to run my fingers over your pure, smooth surface and leave words of love and primal joy in a passionate frenzy," the bully murmured, "well, then, yes, yes, I surely do intend to defile you."

"Oh, my!"

"Oh, my, indeed," said the bully, and he began to write.

And when he was spent, he brushed his fingers over what he had written, and if it was not good, at least it wasn't bad.

"You should not have done that," the page hissed.

At this the bully dropped his facade. "I was just play-acting, lovely page," he cooed, sincerely this time. "If I had and idea you didn't want me to —"

And now the page laughed. "I know, you silly. Two can play that game; in fact, one needs two to, well, tango. Now come here and run your hands over me — oh yeah, like that, that's it —"

"Oh, yes," said the bully.

And then the page struck.

"Ouch!" the bully said, pulling his hand back in pain. "What did you do THAT for?"

"I don't like bullies," said the page.

A LIFTING

He watched the phrases dance across the page.

He heard the melodies. He felt the rhythms. He smelled fresh lilacs and tasted mint. And all the world burst forth from on the page.

Tensions, pent up, eased. His shoulders relaxed, having never sensed their tightness.

The cascading waterfall in his chest slowed to a trickle.

"So, this is peace," he whispered, and was well.

A respite from the rush of frantic need, the quiet nearly overwhelmed him until he sank into it and allowed it to surround his troubled soul, to comfort him with its nothing. He scarcely had noticed the weight until it was lifted, and now this freedom astonished him with its lightness.

He heard the scratch at the corner of his consciousness, and he knew the relief was temporary. One by one, the troubles would settle on his shoulders again, but now he knew what it felt like to shrug them off, and perhaps he would learn to shrug.

A PENNY SEEN

I t was a rainy day, dreary and gray, and so the copper penny was a beacon on the ground against the gray concrete.

The old saying flashed in my mind, "See a penny, pick it up, and all day long you'll have good luck."

I stopped — hesitated would be a better word, because I made no move to pick up the penny. I just saw it down there, registered it in my memory, and moved on across the walk and into the store.

"Somebody else can have the luck," I said to myself. "Could be they need it more."

JASPER

The little beast wriggled in his harness under his jacket. This might not work.

"Name. Town of origin. State your purpose and destination."

He gave the officer the information, hoping she wouldn't notice that his chest was squirming.

Too late.

"What's under your coat — awww, isn't she cute?"

"This is Jasper," he said, hoping she wouldn't look too close.

"Well, you have to declare her, too."

"Him."

"Either way. What breed of cat is he?"

"Oh, he's just a plain, old, domesticated house cat," he said, lying.

"OK, I'll note that," she said, doing so. "You'll have to keep him in that harness for the flight and on a leash always."

"I know. I will."

Thus cleared, he headed toward the aircraft, breathing a little sigh. Well, there's one guard who didn't see the tufts at the end of

Jasper's ears, or didn't care, or didn't know what those ears meant he wasn't a plain, old, domesticated house cat.

The plane's cabin was filled with the usual bustle of people shoving bags into overhead bins and settling into their seats. If external signs were reliable, there were folks from more than a half-dozen countries and probably three continents who had booked passage on this short trip from civilization into the hinterlands. Not that their destination was any less civilized, just less populated and more spread out. He know it would be easier, at their destination, to walk a few meters without having to avoid small collisions with other people. The plane cabin was one last dose of everyday claustrophobia.

The 24-seat jet had only one seat on either side of the center aisle, so there was a degree of separation from his neighbor, a conservatively dressed woman with her hair tamed into a bun. She met his glance as he sat across from her with a polite smile.

He nodded and said, "Hello."

"Hi," she replied and turned back to watching the flight crew scramble about, loading luggage and walking around the plane with officious clipboards. No conversation, then. Fine by him, he wasn't feeling especially talkative.

But then Jasper mewed, fussing a bit. The woman looked over at the sound and her all-business face softened.

"Oh, he's adorable!" she cooed crisply. "You must be planning a long trip if you're bringing your kitty along."

"Not so long," he said, lying. "He just doesn't like to be alone. My neighbors complain he yowls all night when I'm not home."

"Poor baby! It's sweet of you to take him along."

"It's a chick magnet," he said, putting a desperate look on his face. She gave a thin smile and poked at her tablet for something to read. He breathed another little sigh.

Something thumped underneath them, the lights flickered,

and air began to hiss from above them. A mechanical whine started whining, muffled as if coming from the next room, but causing the cabin to vibrate. The sky vessel lurched and began to coast backward, paused, and then rolled forward, turning away from the airport gates.

"Meow," Jasper said, sounding more content than alarmed.

"Yep. Here we go, buddy," he said, bringing his hand up and touching his palm lightly againat the feline's shoulder.

Whatever adventure lay ahead began with this journey.

THE IDIOT

Two men were in the middle of the street, one standing, one in a vehicle.

"You're an idiot," said one, standing.

"Are you calling me an idiot?" said the other, sitting in the parked car.

"You're an idiot," said the standing one from the middle of the street.

"Are you calling me an idiot?" said the other from the car that would be parked in traffic if there were any other traffic.

"You're an idiot," said the first, walking off the street and toward the building.

"You're calling me an idiot?" said the other from the safety of his vehicle.

"You're an idiot," said the first as he walked through the door, and as the door shut behind him, he was heard to say, again, "You're an idiot."

Whether the conversation continued thus, I could not say, for then it was time for me to go my way.

But the words echoes long after, and I wish I knew what prompted the man to insist the other was an idiot — although come to think, he never did clarify to whom he was speaking, so perhaps we intruded on a soliloquy.

MAN AND COMPANION

"I get tired faster than I used to," the old man said. "I remember looking at old people and noticing how they walked, a step at a time, kind of stiff, like everything hurt at least just a little, and lately I've noticed myself walking like that."

"Well, you're old now," said his companion.

"Really? I guess so," said the man. "I do feel old, I guess, some days, and things look a lot fuzzier than they used to when I take off my glasses, and even when I don't. And I find myself saying, 'I'm sorry, what did you say?' more than I did even a little while ago. It bugs me, because I remember impressing a girl when I said, 'Oh, here's Columbia Street,' when we were still half a block away, because I really could read the street sign, my eyes were that good. Yep, I'm feeling old today, no doubt about that."

"I don't know what to tell you," said his companion.

"Me neither, come to think of it," the man said. "It's kind of neat being old. I remember old people talking about how it was when they were kids, and here I am talking about the 1950s and '60s to people whose memories start in the 1980s and '90s or even sooner, and most aren't so impressed, but every so often someone will hear me talking about the first time I saw the brand new Ford Mustang — it was at the 1964 World's Fair, if you want to know — and they'll say, 'That must have been something,' and you can tell they honestly mean it. I said something about the summer of '73 yesterday, and I was gobsmacked to realize that's almost 50 years ago now, and I've lived through three times as many years now as I had then.

"Yep," said his companion.

"Should I be imparting some kind of wisdom here, do you think?" said the man. "I don't really know what I could say. Nobody would listen anyway. Oh, I suppose some might, but wisdom turns out to be something you have to find out for yourself, you know? I'm not sure I even ever found wisdom, and if I did and tried to share it, people would just nod and say, 'That makes sense,' while internally they would be rolling their eyes and not believing it until one day they realize it for themselves. That's the only way anybody learns — for themselves — you know?"

"That makes sense," said his companion.

"And now you're just humoring me," the man said. "Aren't you?"

"Yep," his companion said.

The wind blew, and the snow was falling more urgently now, and it was quiet for a long time.

THE REST AND THE DEAD

"I'll sleep when I'm dead."

Her companion gave her a look that appeared to be somewhat amused, somewhat concerned.

"What an utterly horrid cliche that is," he said.

"What? If I don't get this stuff done, I'm not going to get ahead and we lose the whole account. Or maybe I lose my job."

"And what exactly do you mean, 'get ahead'? Get ahead of what?"

She looked at him coldly. "Do you want me to lose this company? Because that's what could happen if I don't make this customer happy."

"What's so special about this customer?"

"What's so special about any of them? We should treat them all like they're special," she cried. "You never know which one is going to become special."

"All right, all right, you made your point," he said. "All I'm saying is you're only human, and you're working yourself to exhaustion. Everyone needs to rest and recharge sometimes. The world's not going to end if you take care of yourself, and maybe you'll do better with a fresh start in the morning."

She sighed. "Maybe you're right. These numbers aren't making a whole lot of sense anymore. Maybe it's best if I knock off for the night."

"That's the spirit."

"Make sure I don't have any distractions in the morning," she said, straightening her papers and reaching for her briefcase.

"Absolutely."

"And don't let me make any more excuses. We have to finish this by noon."

"You got it."

She walked to the open door, looked back at her desk, nodded, said "OK, then," and walked down the hallway and away.

An unpleasant grin spread over his face, and he reached for the doorknob.

"A little sleep, a little slumber, a little folding of the hands to rest," he murmured, "and poverty will come on you like a bandit and scarcity like an armed man."

His laughter echoed off the barren walls as he closed the door behind her.

WHAT DOES IT MEAN

"What does this mean?" she asked, paging through page after page.

"It's a book, a journal of some sort," mansplained her companion.

"That's obvious," she said, rolling her eyes. "But what does it mean?"

"It means he was arrogant enough to write down his thoughts and ideas for a posterity that doesn't care one whit," he said.

"Or he wanted to record his thoughts and ideas in hopes his future self would understand and remember and know what to do with them," she said more optimistically.

"Maybe that's why anybody writes anything: In hopes the people of the future will remember and understand and know what to do," he said.

"That makes a kind of sense," she said.

"Of course it does," he said smugly. "I said it."

She laughed at that, and he liked the sound of her laugh, and they set the old book aside and kept walking, a step ahead of where they had been before they found the book.

BONES OF A STORY

S omewhere out there, a song was being played, children were dancing, and dogs were contentedly chewing on bones.

Our hero was pensive. She had been planning and waiting, and waiting and planning, and waiting to plan, and planning to wait, and finally the wait was over.

"Today, we act," she told her small cadre of followers — no, "companions" would be a better word, or "colleagues." These were good people but not willing to follow as much as they were willing to cooperate with the plan and collaborate, each for their own reasons, and then go their separate ways — well, except for that one with the gleam in his eye, who was not at all interested in separating when this was done. That was all right; she enjoyed the way they fit together, and their separation was always unwelcome.

And so, they all agreed to act that day.

When it was over, they celebrated, but not with an overwhelming joy, because the battle had taken one of their own, a victory made somber by the loss. Was she relieved that she had survived, and the handsome one with the gleam in his eye? Of course, and she felt a hint of shame that she thought, "At least it was that loss, not this one."

Still, as they held each other that night, they pledged together that the loss would not be in vain, and they would work to ensure the day's victory was a lasting one. It was the best they could do.

WHILE THE CLOCKS TICKED

The wind chimes outside the window protested melodiously as the November wind continued to crash them against each other. The white-haired bearded man pried open his laptop and started to type, as the clock on the left ticked on the backbeat of the clock on the right.

"I should rage against this insane world and the psychopaths trying to ruin it and run it," the old man said, not at all as ashamed of describing himself in the third person as he should be. "The problem is, I'm in a good mood. I should be tired and dragging myself to bed, but I don't feel like sleeping. Not yet."

What was he waiting for? He started at the stuffed snowman smiling down at him behind sunglasses and considered the question. What, indeed, was he waiting for?

"Don't know, don't care," he finally decided. "Tired of waiting. Here I go."

But go where, he wondered?

"Does it matter? A body in motion tends to stay in motion, and so this body needs to keep moving, don't you think?" he cried, to no one in particular because no one in particular was the only other person in the room — the only other person, that is, unless you consider a 16-month-old dog a person.

This day had, in fact, marked the 16-month anniversary of the dog's birth, so she was a few hours into the 17th month of her life. She lay in an adequate imitation of a bear rug on the floor just outside the office where he typed furiously into the night.

"There you go again with the rage and the 'furiously,'" he muttered. "I'm not angry at all, although by all rights maybe I should be. The problem is, the only person I should be angry at is myself."

He pondered the years he thought about saving money toward retirement but always had something else to spend his money on. He thought about his youthful resolution never to buy anything on credit and the pride he felt when he finally dug out of the monstrous hole of debt that had laid him low for literal decades.

"Yeah, but was I smart enough to roll the monthly debt payments into monthly savings payment once the cards were paid off? Nooooo," he groaned. "I was such an idiot."

Still, however, he could not bring himself to get angry or bemoan his fate.

"I'm in too good a mood. So sue me," he said to no one in particular, who continued not to respond.

He looked back up at the snowman again. "You got a problem, Frosty? Why you looking at me like that?"

The snowman smiled back ominously.

"Never, ever call me Frosty again," it said.

"Ooooh, I'm scared," the old man said, not at all afraid, although something nagged at him that he ought to be.

All of a sudden, he lost his train of thought, yawned, and considered the time.

"You know, maybe it wouldn't be such a bad idea to get some sleep after all," he said.

Somewhere in the house, a cat meowed. The wind chimes rang all night. And the snowman kept smiling.

A LONG, LONG TIME

"This isn't the way I imagined it," George Turner said, looking out the window at the blackness. "Are we even moving?"

Yolanda Xenophilius looked at a computer screen. "Yep."

"There's no way to tell for sure. Do you see any movement out there?"

"George," she said. "We're still going 10,833 kilometers per hour. We're still going 3 kilometers per second. Just chill."

"This isn't the way I imagined it," Turner said.

Behind them, a snort.

"You watched too many space movies when you were a kid, George," Jason O'Toole snorted. "You know they put those moving stars in the windows so you could tell the model starships were in motion, right? Real space doesn't look like that."

"Of course I knew," Turner said, sourly. "That's not what I meant."

They lapsed back into silence for a few minutes. Then Sally Ripley, sitting next to O'Toole, started to sing softly.

"Mars ain't the kind of place to raise your kids," she sang. "In fact, it's cold as hell."

"NOT. FUNNY," Turner growled, but his crew mates grinned. "Come on, Sally, stop singing that."

"OK, what would you rather hear?" she said, then began to hum. "Ninety-nine bottles of beer on the wall, 99 bottles of beer …"

That one didn't get quite as much of a guffaw, so she trailed off around 96.

"Are we there yet?" said O'Toole.

It was Xenophilius' turn to scowl, but there was something inauthentic about the scowl.

"Don't make me come back there," she said, and this time even Turner laughed.

They lapsed back into silence for another few minutes. Then Ripley said, "Anyone up for a movie?" They had thousands of choices in the digitized library.

"How about 'Waiting for Godot'?" O'Toole said, and then, "What? Too soon?"

They settled on the film that won the Oscar for Best Picture in 2036. Afterward, they all agreed the Academy was comprised of loons.

"I do think the pelican scene was hysterical," Xenophilius said. "But otherwise …"

"I know, right?" Turner said, but at least he had forgotten his malaise. They grabbed another movie from '36, one that had only been nominated in a couple of technical categories, and had a lot more fun.

When they returned to Earth, they were frequently told they were heroes and so lucky to have been chosen for humanity's first mission to Mars.

"Frankly, I liked the book a lot better," Turner would say.

THE KING OF RANDOM

He sat in the easy chair and spouted random scenes.

"Mr. Random, yep, that's me," he said darkly but with an easy smile. "The story of my life will make no sense. It'll be a new-wave, high-art concept piece, and years from now they'll rave about what a pioneer I was. Yep. I can see it now."

He may have had a cult following had anyone noticed what he was doing, but he was in an out-of-the-way, random place in the internet and no one saw what he was up to.

"It's right clever, though, innit?" he would say to no one in particular, because no one in particular was always there; that is to say, no one was ever there. "Someday they'll see what I was doing, and some high literary critic will say, "My oh my, he was brilliant and we never noticed."

It was always his plan to be discovered and recognized as a genius long after his death, which turned out to be not the greatest plan at all.

Forgotten in his time, he is well-remembered now. For what that's worth.

STARS, MOON AND A SLOW WARMING

She had been in this body for a little more than a year, and the colding time was starting to return. She had trained her human to take her outside, when she gave the signal, to let her deposit waste on the edges of their yard. He always attached a length of cord to her necklace so that they wouldn't be separated, for his safety no doubt, because the wheeled machines that sped along the smooth path up the hill looked like they could be lethal.

Sometimes, before the ceremony of the waste, the two of them would stand side by side in the dark, staring up at the sky or across into the darkness, which was quieter now with the colding on its way. In warmer times they would listen to the cricket and frog song together and contemplate the width and breadth of the universe.

Tonight, after the ceremony, he started toward the door to their abode, but she pulled him toward the smooth path. A short length of smoothness led off the main path and into the abode, and her humans owned two of the lethal machines. They had all ridden together in the machines, which were quite comfortable inside and took them to strange other worlds. The machines reminded her of other vessels, but these did not fly.

She walked her human to the top of the hill, then sat back on her haunches and looked up. The moon near the horizon was due to set in a couple of hours, and stars by the million twinkled in the cloudless sky. He sighed, and she too was overcome by a sad homesickness.

They looked up at the tiny lights in the sky, and he spoke for the first time.

"What do you see out there, girl?" he said. "Do you see your home? Are you from the Dog Star? Lord knows there are times you don't seem like you're of this world."

She raised her eyebrows at that. It was almost as if he knew, but of course he couldn't. For all he would ever know, she was born on this planet, one of many wrigglers who scattered to different homes with different humans, all of them charmed by their wriggliness. They sometimes seemed to suspect, just like her human had just now, but they never really understood. They couldn't.

She was on a mission — a mission to bring peace to a troubled world — a mission that millions before her had been a part of. "Are you from the Dog Star?" He wasn't capable of knowing how close he was to the truth. On the other hand, he did seem to be more intuitive than others of his species, so — no, she was crediting him with too much intelligence.

The Dog Star winked at them from all those light years away, and she had a pang of sadness because she would never be there again.

He sighed again. "Well, let's go back to the house. It's getting cold out here." And she led him back to shelter.

He seemed calmer than he had when they woke that morning. One day at a time, they said. Slowly, slowly, one human at a time, the mission was accomplishing its purpose.

STARS, MOON AND A SLOW WARMING, PART 2

Then one day the man sat down hoping to write a story, and she lay at his feet.

"What shall I write about this morning?" he said to himself. "Another rocket man in love with Mars? A musician who wants to be the next Beatles, who experiments with the music and discovers the sound he always wanted? A reluctant superhero trapped in a world he never made? A dog from another planet who yearns to teach his so-called master the secrets of the universe?"

"There are no secrets," he heard someone say, "only facts of reality you must let unfold so you can see their meaning."

Who had said that? He was alone with his dog. It didn't feel like a thought that originated inside his brain, but the dog was looking at him as if she had said something.

"Was that you, Lily? Am I going nuts?"

Suddenly he felt reassured that he wasn't nuts, and that Lily's name wasn't Lily, and that she was born on a planet circling the Dog Star, and that oh my god no one is going to believe this, and that he wasn't sure he believed it, either.

But Lily only looked at him like she always did, except he would swear she looked gently amused.

MOOSE CALL

S omewhere over my head, I heard the call of a moose.

"Hey!" he called with a flourish. "Watch me pull a rabbit out of my hat."

I rolled my eyes. "That trick never works."

"This time for sure!" he cried. "Here's the secret: Don't think, just write."

"Oh, please," I said. It was close to midnight and a dark and dreary time, while I pondered, weak and weary, over a quaint and curious volume I was attempting to write, and the last thing I wanted was another piece of advice. "You keep coming by to chat, but you always say the same thing — "Don't think!" — but I keep thinking."

"No doubt about it," said the moose, "I gotta get another chat."

So there I was, reaching into the ether, trying to drag a story kicking and screaming into this plain of existence, and the characters were there and the setting was there and the motivations were there, except my own motivation — I didn't care, and if I didn't care, how was I going to get you to care?

"Stop worrying about it," the moose said. "Just write.""

I sighed. "Don't you see that I'm writing?"

"Meh," said he. "Your fingers are moving and words are coming out on the page, but that ain't writing, that's the way you do it."

"What do you suggest?" I challenged.

"I dunno. You're the writer. I'm just a moose."

And with that, he just stopped talking. I have waited here each night since then, waiting for the inspiration, waiting for the moose to speak again. He had to be joking, didn't he? He saw me write, he saw the words come out, how could he say that it wasn't writing? What did he mean by that?

Yeah, that must be it. He was telling a bad joke, trying to make me laugh and start telling the story I was born to tell.

What story is that? I'm glad you asked. Once upon a time ...

The moose grinned. "I guess I don't know my own strength."

All these years I'd been hearing it wrong. It turns out, when I sit down to write, I need to invoke the moose.

THE STORY OF THE COW, THE MOOSE, AND THE GNOME ON THE SHELF

"Cow?" said the gnome.

"What cow?" said the moose.

"That cow," said the storyman.

"Moo," said the cow.

"What was that?" said the gnome.

"It sounded like a cow," said the moose.

"Yes, yes, it was," said the storyman.

"I'm on the shelf above you," said the cow.

"There's a shelf above us?" said the gnome.

"Is it like the shelf below us that we can see?" said the moose.

"Almost exactly, only different," said the storyman.

"We could be friends, I think," said the cow.

"No doubt," said the gnome.

"But we can't see her," said the moose.

"Easily fixed," said the storyman.

"Moo," said the cow.

The storyman plucked the cow from the top shelf and placed her on the middle shelf next to the astonished gnome and the astonished moose, and they became fast friends and stayed that way forever and a day, and after that another day, and after ever on.

BEWARE THE IDES

A public square, people walking, vehicles buzzing past.

"Beware the Ides of September!" cried the old bearded man, boring his wild eyes deep into the stranger's soul, and then, as the stranger stared at him confused, stepped forward and shouted this time: "Beware the Ides of September!"

"Don't you mean March? Caesar's death and all that?" asked the stranger, perhaps a bit condescending, perhaps a bit amused.

"Six months on. The assassins fall in among themselves," said the crazy one. "Your sins shall find you out. Beware the Ides of September."

'Well, I haven't killed any emperors lately," said the stranger, smugly now. "I think I'm safe."

"It's the ones who think they're safe who are in the most danger," the mad prophet snapped. "Beware, I tell thee. Beware the Ides of September!"

"Poppycock," said the stranger, and stepped in front of a dump truck bearing the name Ides & Sons Gravel and Excavating.

LATE ONE NIGHT NEAR A PINBALL MACHINE OVER A GLASS OF WINE

"We are all a little crazy, don't you think? And the fact that we do think is why we don't jump out of the chair and run down the street shrieking, 'You're all crazy, but that's OK because I am a little crazy, too, and it's the only thing that keeps us sane!' We need that little bit of sanity to keep us on the edge instead of toppling over into the abyss.

"We set our goals and make our plans, and then all the pinballs start bouncing off of us and the flippers flip us in another direction entirely. But that's all right, because we learn how to roll with the punches and the collisions that way.

"But seriously, don't you just want to scream sometimes? Are you and I the only ones on the planet who's not nuts? And frankly, I worry about you, because I'm pretty sure I'm a little nuts, too, and you're the only sane one."

As he continued along this merry line of thought, she twirled the wine glass between her fingers and started thinking about exit strategies. This would be very tricky, seeing as how she was married to him, but it would be of no benefit for the room to realize that they belonged together.

"You belong together," they had said. Maybe that was when he started to believe everyone is a little crazy, because he must have seen as well as she did that they did. not. belong. together. He was a bit of a loon — a charming loon, she had to admit, but nonetheless a loon. She was rock solid cool reasoning in a smart and practical dress. But toasts had been toasted and winks exchanged and soothing coos kept cooing that they belonged together.

Maybe it was true, too. But not tonight. Not while he was rambling crazily about how we're all a little crazy and on the verge of screaming down the street.

He stopped rambling long enough to look at her and say, "You're awfully quiet tonight."

And that was true, too, so she shrugged and said, "I guess so."

"Do you know what I guess?" he said after a moment. "I guess there are a million million planets with some form of life or another, and on one of those planets — this very minute! — a couple of beings are having a conversation and one is saying to the other, 'I think this whole thing is crazy, this nutty world where we're always breathing ammonia and sitting on the verge of blowing each other up all the time, but don't those seven moons look beautiful tonight?' That's what I guess." He laughed. "Did you really just roll your eyes at me? You know, you are so cute when you roll your eyes, and I don't blame you. I'm talking silly. I don't know what I'm saying, it's craziness, I sort of feel insane right about now, it's like there's this guy sitting with a beautiful woman and talking about going crazy in this crazy world. I can't blame you for whatever it is you're thinking."

"Do you want to know what I think?" she said.

"Of course I do."

"Do you really want to know what I think?" she said, a little louder.

"What you think is very important to me."

"Do you really, really want to know what I think?" and now she stood and leaned over him, and she was so loud conversations stopped and people turned to hear his answer.

"Why, yes," he said. "I really, really want to know what you think."

She sighed. "I think they were right."

"— about what?"

"We belong together."

His eyes widened. "We do?"

"Yes, we do. I'm crazy about you."

"And I'm just crazy."

The room laughed, even though they weren't joking. But no one went screaming down the street that night, and everyone went home smiling.

THE WRITERS ROOM

He took off his shirt, revealing tattoos scattered across his back in a not-artistic fashion, walked into the water up to his waist, and plunged in. Across the way houses nestled on the side of a hill. Docks and rip rap lined the shore. A pontoon boat waited, moored, ready to be pressed into service on some other sunny day.

His head bobbed as he swam slowly across the river, which was about 200 yards wide at this point. He climbed onto a dock, strode across a deck, slid open a patio door, and stepped inside. A moment later a scream, short and loud, ended as suddenly as it began.

Oh crap, it's too gentle a day to maintain a horror story. What do I do now?

"The characters in a book live day by day and nothing happens," said the woman at the table. "There's no story. They're bored, there's nothing to do here, until one day they realize they're happy having no stories to endure."

One of the men across from her looked up. "That's it?"

"Hey," she said. "Seinfeld did a show about nothing and milked the concept for nine years. Why not do a show with no story?"

"Excuse me," said the little man taking notes at the corner of the table.

"You have to have a story!" insisted the man across from the woman.

"Says who? Stories are overrated," said the woman across from the man.

"Excuse me," the little man tried again.

"Stories are the building block of all we do! You have to have a story!"

"Take your stories and shove —"

"EXCUSE ME!" The little voice was so powerful it hushed the room. Everyone looked at the man with the notepad. "Thank you."

He gathered himself up and assumed his most dignified pose, which, to his credit, had more than a splash of dignity.

"Now then," said the little man, "Who screamed?"

WALK WITH ME

The dog walked over and sat down next to the easy chair, looking up with the sad puppy-dog eyes that dogs have mastered since the beginning of time.

"I'm bored," her eyes seemed to say. "There's nothing to do here. Is this all there is to life?"

"You could read a book," he said with a smile, mimicking what his mother used to say. "You could go outside and play if you promise not to dig up holes and eat plants that make you throw up."

At this the dog took a few steps, circled three times and curled up on the floor, either sulking or drifting off to sleep, or both.

"This does seem to be all there is to life sometimes, doesn't it, Luv?" he said to the dog. "We work for our food and shelter, we keep them and ourselves fit and clean, we pretty up the place a bit, and we entertain ourselves with books and music and TV." He thought about this for a little while. "It's not a bad life. We have enough to get by, if not too much. But you don't want to just 'get by,' do you?

"You want to run through fields and chase the ball for me, race the rabbits through the woods, and step outside the boundaries and see what adventures await out there. I do know how you feel, and I can assure you there is life galore to be had outside these walls and even outside these three lovely acres."

He sat and reflected about some of the life he had led out there, some of it high adventure indeed, some of it happy, some of it very sad.

"Come on, girl," he said to the dog, who jumped right up because she was only pretending to sleep for his sake. "Let's go for a walk."

I would like to say that walk changed everything, that he and the dog lived happily ever after. He did see how much she enjoyed sniffing here way along the field and the street, marveling at everything as if seeing it for the first time — and come to think of it, we are seeing everything for the first time moment by moment, day by day, aren't we? We might change our attitude about life if we saw it all like a dog on a walk.

But for the most part, it was a walk like any other, on a day like any sunny summer day, and in the end it was not memorable, except in the sense that sunny summer days pile up and create an impression that walking along with a dog on a sunny summer day is a pleasant experience that bears repeating, and years from now on a cold winter night, he will think back and remember the summers, and the night won't feel quite so cold.

SOMETHING GOES HORRIBLY WRONG

"I love the feel of paper in my hands," the wild-eyed woman said. "Do you know the feeling? Do you?"

"I know exactly what you mean," the nervous old man said. "Exactly."

"You do, do you?" She said, moving ominously close to him. "Do ya, punk? Exactly?"

"I really think you should take a deep breath," he breathed, "and put down the weapon."

"And all this time I thought you were my friend," the old woman snarled. "All along you were plotting to bring me down."

"That's not true! I mean, yes, I am your friend."

"How do you explain, this morning, how you knew my cat is gone? Did you kill her? Did ya, punk?"

"No, of course not. I heard the news from your neighbor."

"And only the thief would know my necklace was stolen from the drawer in my closet."

"Don't come any closer."

"I'll come as close as I want," she said quietly. "Why are you dead set on making my life miserable?"

"You told me yourself about the drawer in your closet. I just assumed that's where your necklace was stolen from."

"You know what you do when you assume, right? You make an ass out of u and me."

"For the love of God, Agnes!"

The next morning the nice detective came to the door to say her necklace had been found in the stash of a young burglar who had struck several homes in the neighborhood. While they were talking, her cat hopped up on the stoop and rubbed against the detective's leg, back from a long adventure.

"Oops," said Agnes.

BUNNY'S CLOSE CALL

There was a rabbit who lived in a thicket by the side of the road. He loved Ms. Carol's flowers, but she did not return the love.

She liked her flowers just fine the way they were, you see, but the rabbit loved to nibble on them because they were delicious.

One day, the rabbit was munching away when Ms. Carol walked out on her porch carrying a BB gun.

"OK, varmint, that's all the flowers you're going to eat in one lifetime." She took aim and fired.

Fortunately for the rabbit, she didn't aim quite perfectly, and the BB only skipped a pile of mulch into the rabbit's face. This was alarming enough, however, and the rabbit jumped into the air and raced away as only rabbits can race, never to return.

A few days later, Ms. Carol's puppy looked into the empty yard and mournfully back at her.

"I miss the rabbit," the puppy whined.

"Don't you start," she replied. The flowers were pleased, though, and lived happily ever after, or at least for the rest of the bright sunny summer.

TROUBLE IN UTOPIA

In the far-off future year of 2022, in a gleaming city of light, the council met to review its latest scientific goals.

"We have conquered our demons and learned to live in peace," The Leader said smugly. "The worst of our fearful diseases have been eradicated or at least arrested. Our explorers have established outposts on Mars, Venus, and the moons of Jupiter. What's next?"

Suddenly a motley crew burst into the chambers and trained weapons on the wise old men.

"What's the meaning of this?" a council member sputtered.

"While you have been busy making the world a better place, you've neglected the underbelly of society as always," said the motley crew's ringleader. "You've stopped rattling sabers at people we don't know and have no quarrel with, and for that I thank you kindly. And it's very nice that my kids won't die from the disease that killed my mother. It's also good to know I can leave this orb and move to another planet. But I don't want to leave, and there are people still suffering here."

"Suffering? You've just pointed out that no one is at war, we need fear no disease, and opportunities abound on several worlds," The Leader smirked. "Would that we all suffer the like."

"This world is not quite as peaceful as you claim. You didn't conquer our demons, you outlawed them," the ringleader countered. "WHEN HATE IS OUTLAWED, ONLY OUTLAWS WILL HAVE HATE. And, oh, we outlaws have much pent up."

HENRY SAVES THE WORLD

The maguffin was there, in that cave. Of that, he had no doubt.

He stood outside at the entrance triumphantly. No one else knew. He had traced the most obscure clues from ancient time and knew for certain he was at the right spot: There was the marking on the side of the hill, just as described.

He withdrew his gun from its holster, aimed carefully, and fired. The supporting beam cracked, and soil began to dribble from the ceiling, then rocks and boulders amid a great rumbling.

Within seconds the passageway had crashed closed. From here on the side of the hill, it now looked just like a patch of soil. He used his knife to obscure the ancient markings once and for all.

The cave was sealed. The maguffin was buried deep in the mountain where it could never be used again for its evil purposes.

He would sleep well tonight.

LOVELY RITA

When Rita was a little girl, there was a song about a meter maid, and it sounded like such fun, and she grew up to be a meter maid of charm and loveliness, and instead of grousing over tickets people would see her name tag and smile and say, "Oh, it's you! 'Lovely Rita, Meter Maid.' And yes, I suppose I am a little late getting back to my car, and I'll cheerfully pay my fine because you asked so sweetly."

But then they equipped the meters with devices that did Rita's job with electronics and told her "It's not performance-related, it's the economics," and the sadness returned to the meters and the resentment: "I was only a few minutes late, damn machine."

But Rita never lost her smile, and if she were sad not to be walking among her meters – and it did make her sad – she never let on, she just went on to share her charm and her loveliness in other places and for

other people, who said, "You're so lovely, Rita; lovely Rita, you should have been a meter maid."

And she would say, "I was, for a time, but this is now. And I'm so grateful, at least, that I had that chance, for a while."

FOR THE NEXT GENERATION

"This aging stuff is fascinating," the aging man said to his companion. "It's like I'm slowly melting. Everything is falling apart or congealing into a tub of goo, and my mind sees it all happening and is powerless to change the inevitable."

"You could exercise, lose weight, wrap your aching joints, take an aspirin," his companion suggested.

"The inevitable would still be inevitable."

"Of course. But you could delay it, give yourself some extra years to work with."

"There's that," he admitted, sipping his coffee. Rather than set the cup down, he cradled it against his chest, using his prodigious belly as a shelf, feeling the warmth against his fingers. "I want for it to all have meant something, you know? I want to have inspired someone or been a good example. I suppose I could inspire by being a bad example — 'Don't be this guy, children' — but wouldn't it be better to fill others' souls with hope and desire and a drive to greatness?"

"How do you know that hasn't already happened?" replied the companion.

"Wouldn't I know?"

"Maybe, maybe not. Maybe you've written something like It's A Wonderful Life and no one will find it until 30 years from now, you know, maybe that thing you wrote way back when will resonate with the next generation."

"I see what you mean. I'm always digging through old stuff looking for that hidden gem no one has noticed, so I can lift it up and say, 'Look here, isn't this fine? Look at this, listen to that.' And I love when I've been saying that for years and suddenly people have finally seen and heard."

"There you have it," assured the friend. "It's not for you to fully know what you've accomplished, maybe. Maybe someone like you, who searches for the hidden gems, will stumble across your stumbling 50 years from now and think, 'Well, look here, isn't this fine? I need to share this.'"

"I do like to share ..."

MOOSE, GNOME AND COW MEET A SQUIRREL

One day the Moose, the Gnome and the Cow went for a walk. Little white flurries flew, and the waves roared in the bay at the bottom of the hill.

"It's not a fit night out for man nor beast," said the Gnome.

"It's not nighttime, but I agree," said the Moose.

"Moo," said the Cow.

"The weather forecast didn't say anything about snow flurries," said the Gnome.

"Isn't that just like them," said the Moose.

"Mooo," said the Cow.

They walked across the field and past a grove of trees and then a little clearing and finally the woods, where they saw a squirrel.

"Squirrel!" said the Moose.

"It is, that," said the Gnome.

"Moo," said the Cow.

"I ain't seen you around here before," said the Squirrel.

"We've never been this far," said the Gnome.

"That's probably why you never saw us here," said the Moose.

"Moooo," said the Cow, rolling her eyes.

"May I offer you dinner? This is a rough neighborhood," said the Squirrel, holding out an acorn.

"That's very kind of you," said the Gnome.

"What IS that?" said the Moose.

"Mooooo?" said the Cow.

"It's a nut," said the Squirrel. "Haven't you ever seen a nut?"

The Gnome, the Moose and the Cow looked at one another, and looked at the Squirrel, and looked at one another again.

And then they fell to the ground, laughing among themselves.

PROLOGUE TO THE MONARCHS

"Look at that big piece of driftwood," she laughed. "It looks like a dead giant caterpillar washed ashore."

Grant Jenssen laughed, too, but then he took a second look. The wood was washed not quite white, more of a light tan, and the little stubs from broken branches could have been legs; the resemblance to a caterpillar was indeed uncanny except for the fact that it was a meter wide and about three long.

"Wait a minute —"

She saw the look and laughed harder. "Oh, dear, I'm sorry I put the idea in your head. Grant? Oh, please —"

"I have to get down there."

"To look at some flotsam? It's a 10 foot drop or more."

He saw a pile of boulders stacked up to the edge of the cliff a short distance away and, scrambling cautiously, worked his way down to the beach.

"Grant?! Don't be an idiot," she called from above. But he approached the huge bit of not-driftwood in awe.

It was dead, to begin. Certainly no question there. But also, it had once been alive. One. live. giant. caterpillar.

"Where did you come from, little one?" he whispered.

"GRANT!" He looked up and saw her, staring wide-eyed at something in the sky and behind him.

He turned quickly and saw an explosion of orange and black in the sky, hundreds of huge butterflies dancing and swooping in the sun over the water just off shore. They stretched north as far as the eye could see, and the grand dance was clearly making its way south.

For many minutes they passed before them, a procession of monarchs, larger than life, migrating from a place no one could know to a land no one could guess.

And just as suddenly, they were gone, leaving Grant standing alone beside a dead, giant caterpillar and her above on the cliff, laughing and crying like a child.

When sense finally returned to him, Grant thought of the phone in his pocket with its camera, and he cursed himself for being dumbstruck to the point of inaction. More than that, a purpose formed in his soul.

He had to see them again.

A GLIMPSE INTO NOWHERE

"In the town where I was born, an old brick hotel loomed over the downtown. A very long time ago it was a stagecoach stop, with a restaurant and rooms to let, but over the years someone whitewashed it and let it get ugly. Years after I moved away, a new owner sandblasted back to the old brick and made it look lovely again.

"I'm telling you all this to let you know years have passed and much has changed since I left the town where I was born. And actually this is the town where we moved when I was 10; the town where I was born was somewhere else.

"This narrative may be going nowhere, but I have a story to tell that you may or may not want to hear."

The odd old man paused there and closed his eyes. Was he collecting his thoughts or taking a cat nap? The answer would have to wait, because suddenly the session ended, just like that.

AS THE DOGS SLEPT

"Well, you know what they say," he said. "Sleeping dogs lie."

She rolled her eyes. "That's not what they say."

"I'm pretty sure it is."

"OK, fine," she said. "So who's the sleeping dog in this scenario?"

"It's pretty obvious, don't you think?"

"If it was obvious, I wouldn't be asking."

RABBIT HOLE REVENGE

"Hey! What the —" the rabbit said as I tumbled onto his head.

"Sorry, bun," I said. "How did I get here?"

"I am so over people like you," said the rabbit, his whiskers twitching. "You fall into my hole, eyes all glazed, rude as can be, land on my head or wake up my kids, and you have the nerve to ask, 'How did I get here?' You know dang well how you got here. You're just too embarrassed to say."

These last few words were accompanied by a series of strong finger jabs to my chest. And before you try to tell me rabbits don't have fingers, let me point out that rabbits also don't talk.

"Honestly," I said apologetically, "I'm as surprised as you are."

"Then you're not surprised at all," the rabbit sniffed, and sniffed again. "What did you think would happen? You pick up that insidious device all the time, knowing it can send you down a rabbit hole, and you scroll and scroll until you find a perfect little rabbit hole to dive down. Well, enough is enough. Come on, guys!"

All of a sudden I was surrounded by rabbits. Drumming

started to thunder out of the walls, and the rabbits began to sing along with a jangling electric guitar.

"We're not gonna take it, no, we ain't gonna take it, we're not gonna take it anymore," they sang as they swarmed over me.

I will probably post a link to this story, like always, but as I glance over at my iPhone and contemplate opening Facebook, I break out in a sweat, remembering the hordes of vengeful furry animals crawling on my chest and weighing me down, shouting Twisted Sister in my face.

My therapist says with a few years of hard work, I may be able to function normally again. But in the meantime, I can't go out in the backyard.

There are bunnies out there.

CLIFF'S NOTES NOVEL

The journey was epic, but the Woodywacs finally made it from one place to another.

The reason for the journey is lost to the ages. Were they leaving their ancestral home to find a new homeland, or were they returning home? No one knows. They just know that the epic journey was made and the Woodywacs have called Woodywacacia home for the ensuing centuries.

Would they ever leave Woodywacacia again? The Woodywacs would tell you there was no need — the land is fertile and generous, so only a catastrophe could make them move.

Enter Katastrofee, goddess of malice. She swooped in one day and burned the crops and earthquaked half the village to rubble.

But the Woodywacs gathered round and drove her away, if not forever, then for the foreseeable future, and they lived happily ever after although ever vigilant for the return of Katastrofee.

NO NEWS IS GOOD NEWS

He turned on the television to find anchors engaged in the everlasting search for the world's bad stuff, compiling a log of people doing harm to one another, nature's fury wreaking havoc on innocents, death and destruction both accidental and intentional, and, of course, members of the ruling class throwing insults, half-truths and outright lies at one another.

"How can you tell he's lying? His lips are moving," one liar shouted.

"She wouldn't know the truth if it bit her in the nose," sneered another.

An explosion and fire in a country half the world away. A mother drives herself and two children into a lake 500 miles from here. Random shootings and rioting in the streets 750 miles away. A gruesome vivisection 1,003 miles from downtown.

The anchor raised his hand toward the camera and said, "With pandemic news, economic shutdowns, and partisan battles, you might be thinking, 'Things can't possibly get any worse.' Well, brace yourself for what's next. After the break, balanced coverage of last night's incident in the southern part of the state that some are calling the most brutal they've seen in many years — and why the owner of this small business in Timbuktu says he's calling it quits. Stay with us."

"No!" he shouted back at the television. He turned it off and looked out the window. "What's wrong with people, Maude? When we were kids you didn't have all this going on."

"Oh, yes, we did, Ted," Maude said. "There've always been wars and rumors of wars, and people who hated each other, and there's always going to be. It's in the Bible even, isn't it?"

"We didn't have TV telling us all the time, like this," Ted said. "Even the good news is bad. 'The economic is booming, but it could get worse any time now,' that's what they say, I'm telling ya."

"Let's keep the TV off and just live our lives, then," Maude said.

Over the next month or so, Ted and Maude came and went as they pleased, enjoying each other's company, sunrises and sunsets, and the changing of the seasons. Sometimes they found themselves in a rainstorm without an umbrella, but otherwise they didn't miss the litany of horror, hate and mayhem hanging over everyone else, every morning and night for years.

Saying "happily" may be a stretch, but they lived calmly and serenely ever after.

THE ROOM AFTER LIFE

The caffeine delivery system wasn't working as efficiently as normal. Here was the soothing hot water with its familiar taste warming the back of his mouth, but the morning fog wasn't lifting. The jolt of go-get-them wasn't jolting. It all just didn't seem as urgent as before.

The events of the last 48 hours hardly seemed real. The visit by the mysterious stranger, the delivery of the unbelievable package, and the struggle for sanity – it all melted into one confusing ball that seemed beyond his reason to suss out.

He took another sip of the coffee, then buried his upper lip into the mug to pull in a full gulp. Come on, brain, he commanded silently, make all this make sense. If the puzzle wasn't solved by 10 o'clock this morning, the courier would go back without what they were demanding of him, and the game would be lost.

That was the problem, then: Mustn't lose the game. As if lives were not at stake, the players all spoke of "the game." The rules of the game. The need for sportsmanship. No, no, you can't steal people's lives that way – there are codes of conduct that must be followed. Fuck this game. He wanted to go back to sleep. A little rest, a little folding of the arms to catch his breath, and maybe this would all go away, no more worries, no more – pain.

That's odd. Where was the pain coming from?

He'd been sleepier than he realized. Only now did he remember the fight of the night before, when he had fought to the death and – well, he'd fought to the death and lost.

This must be the afterlife.

"I didn't think it'd be so comfortable," he said. And it was, at that. Someone had left him a cup of coffee, the hound was at his feet, and outside the spring morning birds were providing a song for the ages.

"Everything is to your satisfaction, then, sir?" The valet had come up quietly from behind, even though this chair had been against a wall all of his life.

"Well, except for the being-dead part, yeah, I feel pretty satisfied," he said.

"That part's out of our control," the valet said. He was an androgynous sort – could have been a she and come to think of it, maybe she was. The room and the air had a sexlessness to it, if such a thing could be said. There were no touches that would make the room masculine or feminine, except perhaps for the manly mug that held the coffee.

"Do I even need coffee anymore?"

"Need is such a tricky word," said the valet. "If it brings you comfort, well then, yes, you need coffee now more than ever."

"And where is this place? What time is it? What do I do with myself, being dead and all?"

"Ah," said the valet. "Here is the moment when you realize there never was anything behind this concept you and the others have called 'time.' Time doesn't pass, and 5 o'clock doesn't exist. Everything just is. As to where you are and what you do with yourself, that's all up to you."

"Of course there's time," he said. "There was the time before I was here, and there will be the time after this conversation. Time passes. Things happen. We measure the before and the after."

The valet looked on quietly and patiently.

"Will there be anything else, sir?"

"I'd like another cup of coffee, please –" and then he saw that his mug was full of hot, brown beverage. "Oh. I see."

"This place does have its advantages," the valet winked.

THE MAN WHO WAS AFRAID OF FINISHING

Finnegan Moore was good at starting things, but he seemed to have a phobia about endings, completions. It was if he believed that endings were little deaths, as if finishing a book was a good time to die, or finishing a work project, or the last film in a trilogy, or the last show of a series – and he didn't want to die.

"Lord, let me live to see how the story ends," was a constant refrain of his life. He was relieved to reach the end of the Harry Potter stories, but also terrified, because now that he knew how the story ends, would someone in the sky decide it was now an appropriate time to take him?

"But you know how the story ends," his friend Dan said one day. "You know how everyone's story ends – with an ending, and not necessarily wrapped up in a bow."

"That's just it, you see," Finnegan said. "That's just it. I'm afraid of finishing because it's a little death."

"Are you afraid of sleep? Some poet once described sleep as a little death and –"

"I'm afraid of not waking up," Finn allowed. "And sometimes

I'm afraid of waking up, too. Afraid of what my waking hours will bring."

"Afraid of dying, and afraid of living," Dan said. "Afraid to start and afraid to finish. 'Fear not,' said the angel. Don't be so afraid, Finnegan."

"But I think that may be at the core – being always afraid. It's like fight or flight, and it's always been my choice to run away from the ending – that is, when I'm not running away from getting started."

"So your resolution, then, is to choose fight over flight this year," Dan suggested. "When the urge to walk away rises up, you face down the hungry wolf eying your fat, juicy self and fight for your life."

"Meaning I finish what I've started."

"There you go."

"How long do you think this will last?" Finnegan said. "I don't follow through on resolutions very long."

"Knock it off. Of course days will come when you don't do what you said – or at least days when, it the past, you would let it slide. If it slides, well, don't let it happen again. But don't declare failure at the first slide, or even the second or third. Keep going until you don't slide. Don't leave the bike on the ground; pick it up and start riding again."

"There are a lot of mixed metaphors in this conversation," Finn said.

"Mixed or not, keep the lights burning. Don't worry," Dan said. "A good metaphor – even a mediocre metaphor – is good for the soul."

"So what's next?" Finnegan said hopefully. "Do I march forward, pick something undone and finish it, or do I start something new and follow through to the end?"

"You know the answer is yes," Dan smiled. "Yes – do one, and then the other, or chip away at both until complete. Measure your progress, though, so you can see it moving along."

"Thanks, Dan," Finnegan said.

"Thank yourself. I'm just a figment of your imagination anyway," said Dan. "But always remember the power of the imagination is unlimited."

"Happy New Year, Dan," Finnegan said.

"That's up to you," Dan whispered, and was gone.

THE PLACE HOLDER

The custodian pulled out his keys with a jangle, fiddled for the one, and opened the door.

A man was sitting on the battered leather couch, staring into a smartphone screen.

"Who are you, then?" the custodian said. "You're not Mr. Comfort."

"No, no, I'm not," the man on the couch said. The custodian looked toward the other door. "She's not here, either."

"Well, what's all this, then? And what are you doing in this office?"

"I'm the place holder."

"The what?"

He finally looked up from the smartphone.

"I'm the place holder," said the place holder. "Once upon a time there was this writer, and he made a pledge to write a story every week and give it to the world on a Saturday morning. One week, something went horribly wrong. Except it didn't, you see."

"Something's horribly wrong but it isn't? What's that supposed to mean? And how did you get in here?"

"Oh, he gave me a key. I put it back on the desk."

The custodian looked at the desk. Sure enough, there was a key in the middle of the blotter.

"Well, you know about the stories, then," he said, somewhat mollified. "Are you trying to tell me there's no story?"

"Oh, there's a story," the stranger said. "The story is you and me. How well do you know the writer?"

"I've been cleaning here twice a week for 20 years," the custodian said.

"Good. Now here's the point: Has he ever made a promise, like the one to write a story every week, and then not followed through?"

The custodian blushed. "Well, yeah." Before the man with the smartphone, who had a look of smirky triumph on his face, could respond, he added, "But he was following through big time. He's been writing up a storm all week, talking under his breath with a big smile on his face. He was really looking forward to putting out his story this morning, and now you're saying it ain't here?"

"Not that story," the intruder said. "He tore out his hair last night and said, 'Goodness goose! It won't be ready!'"

"Yeah, that's something he might say," the custodian muttered. "So the story is just you and me talking about how there's no story?"

"Pretty much."

"That ain't too much of a story, is it?"

"Not really. He left this post, telling people if they still want one of his stories, they can look through the older ones under the link over there on the left that says 'Stories,'" he said, displaying the post on the screen. "It says he's so excited about the new story, he wants to finish it off properly before he puts it out there. Then he wrote a story about a custodian finding a place holder in Mr. Comfort's office."

"He promises a new story every Saturday and then dashes something off in 20 minutes, doesn't even show up and leaves a note that says, 'You can always check out the old stories.' Ain't that just typical."

The two men looked at each other in silence for several seconds. Then the man with the smartphone pushed himself up off the couch.

"Well, we've managed to talk for more than 500 words," the place holder said. "You reckon that's enough? Let's go for a drink."

The custodian looked around the office. "I still have cleaning to do."

"Right," the place holder snorted. "And he still has writing to do."

"Yeah, good point," said the custodian. "Let's get out of here."

ON THE EDGE OF CONSCIOUSNESS

Birds sing outside, trees sway in the breeze, and I sigh with over-pouring memories of warm hugs and wild embraces, earnest conversations about lofty notions, and a quest for happily ever after.

As soon as I realize I am in the poetry zone, I surface for air. "No, no," I cry, "I want to drown in there. I want to bask in the words and find new combinations to turn the keys of locked hearts and open them to possibilities."

I only brushed against the immersion for a moment, but what I saw ignited a hunger for more. As I pack my suitcase, I feel a determination unlike any I have felt before. I will find the place where treasures lie, I will pick them up and polish them to a sheen, and then I will share them with whoever seeks peace and love and foolish cliches and nonsensical worlds beyond this one.

THE HOUND AND THE HUMAN

"Sometimes I look out the window and see the life racing by, or sliding by, or drifting by, or hopping along, or fluttering this way and that, or waving in the wind, and I think, 'Is this all there is?'" said the philosophical hound.

"You know what your problem is?" asked her human.

"No opposable thumbs?"

"Well, besides that. Your problem is you don't see there are two sides to the window. Life isn't just out there; it's in here, too."

"It looks pretty static."

"That's because there aren't as many critters in here."

"And that's my point. Most of the living is being done out there," said the hound.

"Whoa," realized the human. "You're right. We're blocked off from life in here."

"Shall I invite some of them in?"

"No, no, no, that's why it's called shelter. But we need to go outside and encounter some life out there, as well as in here."

"I usually need to go outside and do some business."

"Well, er, that, too."

"You're lucky," the hound said. "You have a special room for that."

"Or I'm unlucky," countered the human, "because it's so easy to insulate myself in here and never go out among the other life forms."

"I have to agree, there are a lot of interesting things to see out there," said the hound. "You live a strange life, staring at glowing objects and paper containers and listening to unusual sounds while you sit stationary in an easy chair. What do you see in those things?"

"In their own way, those are windows to the outside world, too," the human mused.

"So we're the same in that sense," said the hound. "We sit by the window and watch the life go by, when we could be living."

"Excellent point," the human said. "OK, what do you say, girl? Shall we go for a walk?"

"I was thinking ride," said the hound, "but a walk with do."

JACKPOT

(**B**
The place was a dive. Old photographs of famous people who once ate there hung on the walls, but none of the pictures was newer than somewhere in the mid 1970s. Faded wallpaper was starting to peel at the seams. The place smelled somewhere between a campground latrine and the morning after a frat house party.

A man in a trench coat and wearing a fedora — God, could he be any more of a cliche? — slid into the booth opposite him.

"You Slate?" the stranger said, his hands visibly trembling before he folded them to keep them still.

"I suppose so," Slate said. "And you are —?"

"Doesn't matter."

"OK, have it your way, Doesn't Matter. What's this about?"

"Have you ever seen a TV show called *The Blacklist*? FBI teams up with a mysterious crime lord, they end up using each other, and there's this girl agent —"

"No. Never saw it."

"Doesn't matter. It's just, there's this one episode —"

Slate straightened up. "You called me down here to talk to me about an old TV show? Are you kidding me?"

"It's not that old, just a few years back —"

"Get to the point. Now."

"It's real," the trembling man said. "This one episode, it's not just a story, it's real."

"Yeah, they do that all the time. 'Based on a true story.' I can't believe I'm wasting my time with this."

"In this one story, this guy uses DNA to find people who are prone to violence, and then he manipulates their life to trigger them. This one lady shoots up a bank, and another guy goes off on a high-speed chase and pulls a gun on cops after he crashes and —"

"'Based on a true story,' huh?"

"He does things like that to manipulate them, screws with their lives until they snap. I watched it on Netflix the other night and wrote down the formula."

"There's a formula for turning people into killers," Slate said flatly.

"Don't be sarcastic, man, yes, there is," Doesn't Matter said, unfolding a piece of paper and pushing it across the table. "Here, take a look."

The writing was as much of a scrawl as Slate expected, but not as hard to read as he thought it would be.

FIRST PHASE: DISRUPTION OF SCHEDULE, ROUTINE, DAILY LIFE

SECOND PHASE: DESTABILIZE SENSE OF SELF-WORTH

FINAL PHASE WAS TO SEVER THE PRIMARY EMOTIONAL BOND

GET ALL THREE, JACKPOT

"This is the formula?" Slate asked.

"Yeah. Don't you get it?"

"Enlighten me."

The man pulled a cigarette from a rumpled pack and fiddled with it as if he would pay a million bucks for the courage light it up.

"Come on, look around you," he said. "Last few months, everybody's routine has been screwed up. Places closed down, people told to stay home. The new normal is that nothing's normal. And if you don't like it, they tell you how stupid you are, dump on your self-esteem, you know?"

Slate snorted. "It's a big government conspiracy, is it? They want to drive everyone to violence — whoever 'They' is. And you dragged me down here to ask me to — what?"

"Haven't you noticed how crabby people are nowadays?" Doesn't Matter said, his eyes wide beneath the fedora. "One more push, maybe one after that, and we're all gonna blow."

Slate stared across the table.

"You're right," the trembling man said, tossing the shredded cigarette onto the floor and rising. "There's nothing you can do, nothing anyone can do. I don't know why I called you."

"Well, I'm glad I could help you get it off your chest."

"Yeah."

The man took off his fedora, withdrew a small pistol from the hat, and shot the television set above the bar. As people scattered, he took four hundred-dollar bills out of his pocket and tossed them on the counter.

"Sorry about the mess," he said, and walked into the night.

Slate left town the next morning. He was well off the grid,

camped out in a safe place, when the serious stuff started happening.

THERE WAS THIS STORY

"Why did you tell me this story, old man?"

The young man seemed agitated, the old man calm.

"What do you mean by that?"

"Just answer the question," the young man said. "Did you think I would learn something? Did you want to warn me about something? Did you wish to frighten me? inspire me? belittle me?"

"I had no such intentions," the old man said, a little too strenuously. "I just wanted to tell you a story."

"Why that story? Why tonight?"

"It seemed like this night was the right night for this story."

"Why?"

"Well – I suppose I don't know why, exactly," the old man said. "I just felt the sinews of this evening and started to tell. Before I knew it, it all was told."

But they both knew. The story loomed over them, surrounded them, convicted them, and ultimately changed them. And the most sobering thing was: The story could never be untold.

ABOUT THE AUTHOR

Warren Bluhm (1953-) was raised in New Jersey but fell in love at first sight with the blue skies of Wisconsin, where he has spent his entire adulthood, first in radio news and more recently as a reporter/editor of community newspapers.

He writes reflections, stories and books that aim to encourage, entertain, and enlighten, sometimes one more than the others.

Warren lives near the shores of Green Bay with his beloved golden retrievers, Dejah Thoris Princess of Mars and Summer.

FICTION
Dejah & Summer in the Time of Magic
Ebenezer: A sequel of sorts to A Christmas Carol
Myke Phoenix: The Complete Novelettes
The Imaginary Revolution
The Imaginary Bomb

NON-FICTION
A Declaration of Peace
Refuse to be Afraid
It's Going to be All Right
Echoes of Freedom Past
Full: Rockets, Bells & Poetry
Gladness is Infectious

How to Play a Blue Guitar
A Bridge at Crossroads
A Scream of Consciousness